CARRIAGE FOR TWO

When Judith Taverner and her young sister, Bess, are left penniless, clearly a wealthy husband has to be found for Bess. Mr. Aidan Carrock seems to be ideal; after all, he is considered the most eligible man in the district. However, Judith's plans are complicated by the arrival of a new neighbour, the attractive Mr. Mardale, and she is horrified to find herself falling in love — or is it simply infatuation?

CUMMINS, M.   F

Carriage for two

N.B

AF

30/3/17

19 . . . 2008   0 8 JAN 2008

1 7 MAR 2008   M J c

1 6 APR 2008   1 0 FEB 2009

ALBEMARLE 1 3 MAY 2008   1 3 MAR 2009

Davies   2 5 SEP 2015

1 3 JUL 2012

0 8 JUL 2014

This item is to be returned or renewed on or before the latest date
above. It may be borrowed for a further period if not in demand.
To renew items call in or phone any Warwickshire library, or renew
on line at www.warwickshire.gov.uk/wild

Discover • Imagine • Learn • *with libraries*

www.warwickshire.gov.uk/libraries

1 0 JUL 2015

Warwickshire County Council

1 2 NOV 2014

EM

MARY CUMMINS

◆

CARRIAGE
FOR TWO

Complete and Unabridged

LINFORD
Leicester

First published in Great Britain in 1984 by
Robert Hale Limited
London

First Linford Edition
published 1998
by arrangement with
Robert Hale Limited
London

British Library CIP Data

Cummins, Mary
    Carriage for two.—Large print ed.—
Linford romance library
    1. Love stories
    2. Large type books
    I. Title
    823.9′14 [F]

    ISBN 0–7089–5238–0

Published by
F. A. Thorpe (Publishing) Ltd.
Anstey, Leicestershire

Set by Words & Graphics Ltd.
Anstey, Leicestershire
Printed and bound in Great Britain by
T. J. International Ltd., Padstow, Cornwall

This book is printed on acid-free paper

1

THAT morning Mrs. Armstrong had packed her bags and Miss Judith Taverner had arranged for Joss Peters to take her to the railway station at Cockermouth from whence she could begin her journey to London. Miss Elizabeth Taverner retired to her room in tears.

"I do not know what we are going to do, Judith," she said. "Everyone is deserting us. There is only Nanny left now. And Joss."

"Nanny is family," said Judith, briskly, "and I say good riddance to Mrs. Armstrong. She made our mother's life a misery with her endless complaints and her sarcastic remarks which left us in no doubt about how other people could manage their affairs so much better than ourselves. She was wasteful in the kitchen, too."

1

"But there is no one to cook for us."

Judith sighed and looked thoughtfully at her young sister. It was hard for Bess to adjust to the tragedy which had overtaken them. Both their parents had been killed when their coach overturned on a mountain road only six miles from their home at Greyfells, which overlooked Bassenthwaite Lake. Elizabeth had been at school in Appleby, but fortunately Judith, at eighteen, had already finished her education and her father, John Taverner, was already making plans to find a husband for her.

"We must arrange for Judith to meet several young men," Lucy Taverner had entreated. "She should marry for love, my dear."

"Judith is a sensible girl," John Taverner said, gruffly. "I've brought her up to be sensible. We cannot set her up too comfortably. But she is well educated and there have been Taverners at Greyfells for over two hundred years. She bears an old and honoured name. She will marry a man of substance. Bess, also."

"Bess is soft and gentle. She will need a man who loves her and is happy and willing to take care of her. She is . . . "

"Like her mother," John Taverner had said, putting a hand over his wife's. "Rest assured, my dear, that our little Bess will be cared for when the time comes."

There would always be someone to take care of Bess, John Taverner had thought with a sigh. His investments had not been doing well of late, and he had speculated with money which had hitherto made a small but steady profit from gilt-edged stock. Unfortunately, his bid to recoup losses had not been very successful, and John was faced with a trip to London to consult his broker. Lucy had insisted upon accompanying him on the journey, leaving Greyfells in the capable hands of Judith. Sometimes she worried that Judith had not wanted to leave Cumberland and spend a season in London, but had been easily persuaded that the money was likely to be wasted.

"I could not live without sight of the mountains and lakes, Mama," Judith protested. "Besides I am not a beauty . . ."

"Nonsense," said Mrs. Taverner, though her quick response bore a note of falsity. Judith's looks were too unusual to be classified as beautiful. She was tall and gentlemen preferred small, dainty ladies. Her hair was beautiful, long, luxurious and naturally curly, but it was very dark brown and her eyes were blue. Mrs. Taverner thought that Judith's eyes were often fearless and even bold when she was confronted with a problem, and gentlemen preferred shy gentle looks from a young lady. Bess was still young, but already her lovely fair hair, delicate complexion and forget-me-not blue eyes attracted attention. It would be well to marry Judith to some nice eligible man before Bess grew old enough for marriage, otherwise the young men would prefer the younger sister.

She looked at Judith. "Your father says you are very handsome, my dear," she said, honestly. In fact he had said that Judith would still be a beauty if she lived to be ninety.

"I do not care, Mama," said Judith, smiling. "I love Greyfells. I want to stay here for the rest of my life."

She often stood in the wide bow window of the drawing room from whence she could look out across the distant Bassenthwaite Lake to the towering heights of Skiddaw beyond. Judith vowed that the mood of the mountain changed every day. Sometimes it was pale misty blue in the haze of a warm summer day, then the sky would darken and the mountain became purple and gold, a never-ending enticement to the stalwart gentlemen who dared to challenge her peaks.

John and Lucy Taverner had never made their journey to London. News was brought to Judith that their coach had overturned and both her parents had been thrown on to the hard mountain road. Judith had known little about her father's affairs, but over the next few months she had learned much. Her father's solicitors had their offices in Carlisle and old Mr. Brent had tried to break the news of their sad situation as gently as possible. His nephew, young Mr. Brent, who was almost as old as John Taverner had been, advocated the sale of Greyfells, but Judith had refused to contemplate such an idea. Their servants had been paid until the end of their term, and Judith had written out good references to enable them to find new employment. Mrs. Armstrong, the housekeeper, had been kept on, also old Nanny Sherman, who had nowhere to go, and Joss Peters whose father had also lost his life in the accident. Joss and his mother lived in the coach-house, and Joss had pleaded to be allowed to stay for his mother's sake. Mrs Peters did not want to leave the security of her home. Judith had negotiated Joss's wages, and he declared himself satisfied and offered to do any work required of him.

Judith sat up into the long hours of the night working out facts and figures, and she decided that she and Bess could live very frugally on the income which would be theirs, but sooner or later something would require to be done. She might be willing to forego new gowns and entertainment of any kind, as well as helping Joss with the vegetable garden or crimping Bess's lace if Nanny felt too tired, but Bess would feel ill-used if she were asked to put herself forward for such tasks.

She would have to find a husband for Bess, thought Judith, having brought her young sister home from school in Appleby, and seen how easily Bess could become bored now that her noisy grief had abated.

Judith had not shed tears for her parents. The wound of their loss was so deep and hurtful that she had tried to ignore it and put it out of her thoughts. Nothing else was bearable. Instead she concentrated on the business of staying alive and holding on to as much as was familiar to her as possible. She could live under these circumstances, she assured herself, but not Bess.

In fact, it was very difficult to explain to Bess why they could not now have everything to which they had been accustomed in the past, and it was largely through Bess's petulant demands that Mrs. Armstrong had decided to pack her bags, and in fact, had been encouraged to do so by Judith.

"Miss Elizabeth expects me to work miracles in the kitchen, Miss Judith," she sniffed. "She will not have eggs and she is bored with lamb, and I am sure the vegetables which Joss brings in are not what I have been used to. In fact, nothing here nowadays is what I've been used to. Nanny Sherman is no help. She just gets in my road, and to hear her you would think she was a best quality servant when . . . "

"When she has only served the Taverners of Greyfells for the past forty years," said Judith, quietly, "and we are certainly not the quality you are used to, Mrs. Armstrong. It does seem unfortunate that our neighbours, Mr. and Mrs. Hugo Carrock of Burroughs Park only required your services for such a short time when you travelled north from London. My mother agreed to employ you when Mr. Hugo died and Mrs. Carrock went to London. Perhaps the new heir, Mr Aidan Carrock would have been more to your liking if he had come home to take up his inheritance, but Burroughs Park is still being run by an estate manager and is without a mistress."

Mrs. Armstrong looked sour.

"Though I understand you were not

employed there as housekeeper," Judith continued. "I seem to remember my mother mentioning this."

Mrs. Armstrong's face coloured. "I may not have been housekeeper at Burroughs Park," she said, "but they was the *real* Quality. They did not have to pinch and scrape up the last penny to pay me."

"Nor shall I," said Judith, silkily. "I would not deprive you of the chance to serve in a household of better quality. Tomorrow Joss will be pleased to drive you to Cockermouth where you can take the train to Penrith and thence to London. I will pay your fare and all monies due to you, of course, until the end of the term. I doubt if a reference from Miss Taverner of Greyfells would be of sufficient help to you when you apply for another position, but I will write one for you, if you so wish. Meantime, Mrs. Armstrong, my sister and I will be happy to eat what you have cooked for dinner this evening. Miss Elizabeth is lying down and I have some oddments which my father had set aside to be handed in at the vicarage for the annual garden fête. I will be back within the hour."

The colour had ebbed from Mrs. Armstrong's face but she turned away with a sniff.

"Just as you like, Miss, though you will need me before I need you."

"I think not," said Judith, quietly.

Anger was biting into her. She knew that her temper was not of the best and had worked hard to control it over the years, but Mrs. Armstrong set her teeth on edge. When she was old enough to see how much the woman patronized her rather gentle mother who was not too competent at running Greyfells, Judith had begun to find the housekeeper irritating, but she did her work well and competently. It was only the studied lack of respect in her manner which could be faulted.

Now she was on her own, thought Judith, as she walked along the winding drive with the rhododendrons already

11

in bud and the daffodils in full bloom. The narrow road wound down a hillside towards the small Norman church and the vicarage, which had been built in the days of Queen Anne. The Reverend Stephen Laird would no doubt be busy about his sermon for Sunday but his wife, Agnes, being ten years his junior and not yet thirty, was young enough to be a friend for Judith, yet old enough to give her sensible advice. She had never needed it more, thought Judith, as she swept her long black skirt through the small gate which led to the back of the house. At this time of day she was most likely to find Mrs. Laird in the kitchen.

* * *

Agnes Laird wore a large white apron to protect her pretty gown of lavender and white checks, and she was busily instructing a young girl, also enveloped in a white overall with a matching white cap to protect her hair, in the intricacies of mixing a rich fruit cake.

She turned to look out of the window as Judith tapped lightly on the kitchen door, then went to open it with a smile of welcome on her pleasant face.

"Miss Judith! Do come in . . . " Agnes Laird began to remove the apron.

"No, do not allow me to interrupt you, Mrs. Laird," Judith protested. "That is precisely why I come to the kitchen door. I am happy to sit on a chair and perhaps learn a little as you teach young Maisie."

"Your place is hardly in the kitchen, Miss Judith," Agnes Laird smiled.

Judith sighed. "Perhaps I shall spend little time anywhere else from now on. Mrs. Armstrong leaves us in the morning."

Mrs. Laird's eyes were keen and she turned briskly to Maisie Neill who had poured the cake mixture into a prepared tin."

"Into the oven with this, then, Maisie, but before we tidy the kitchen, please bring a tray of tea for Miss Judith and myself to the drawing room. We shall all have a rest. I think we have earned it."

"I have brought along the books and bric-a-brac which Father promised to Mr. Laird for the fête. Where shall I put the box?"

"Let me take it. Goodness, Miss Judith, it is quite heavy. Surely Joss could have brought it."

"It did me good to carry it," said Judith. "I needed to walk to smooth down a few prickles."

The drawing room was small compared with Greyfells, but it was warm and cosy and a large log fire burned brightly in the fireplace. Mrs. Laird was a good housewife, thought Judith, looking at the well-polished plain furniture. The carpet was worn and the curtains had been neatly patched in places, but this did not detract from the charm of the room.

Judith had always loved her home and had taken the cleanliness and comfort of it very much for granted, but gradually she was becoming afraid of what was happening to her and Bess. Suppose she could not keep Greyfells clean. Nanny could not help. She was too old. And although she had two girls to help her from Burroughs village, they were not well-trained like Maisie. Mrs. Armstrong had pointed out their faults but had failed to show them how to do their work properly.

Judith supposed she ought to do that herself, but she hardly knew where to begin, yet she hesitated to ask Mrs. Laird for help. The vicar's wife already had a great deal of parish work to do in order to help her husband with his duties.

"Cheer up, Miss Judith," she encouraged. Agnes Laird was full of sympathy for both young ladies from Greyfells, but especially for Miss Judith. Few people had realised that the Taverners of Greyfells were living in reduced circumstances. It was very hard that the young ladies should lose their parents, but to lose their security also was a very heavy blow.

She poured out a cup of golden China tea, and added a slice of lemon.

"Please try one of Maisie's biscuits."

"She must be a great help to you, Mrs. Laird," said Judith. "I will try to train my maidservants. I cannot bear that Greyfells should become neglected."

"You must encourage Miss Elizabeth to help," said Mrs. Laird, crisply. "If she learns to supervise your housemaids, then you can advise and guide Joss. You could manage quite competently."

"You know very well that we will only be able to manage adequately," said Judith, "but there is no need for you to be concerned, Mrs. Laird. I shall gain experience, I am quite sure, and after that we will manage very well."

"I will help you in any way I can," Agnes Laird offered.

Miss Taverner was a proud young woman, but she was realistic enough to accept help in a sensible manner, thought Mrs. Laird. What a pity she had not been married when the tragedy happened. But there were so few eligible men in the neighbourhood, and Mr. Aidan Carrock was a complete stranger to all of them. He had lived abroad for several years, but now . . .

"He is coming home," Mrs. Laird murmured her thoughts aloud.

"Who is coming home?" asked Judith.

"Mr. Aidan Carrock. The Vicar has received notification, also Joseph Webb and his wife, Nancy, have been given their instructions to open up Burroughs Park and the housekeeper, Mrs. Whitaker is employing servants from the village."

"Does he bring his wife with him?" asked Judith, her interest suddenly sharpened.

Mrs. Laird's eyes flickered. What was behind the question? Miss Taverner was a fine young lady, but not quite the match for the heir to Burroughs

Park. If she were thinking that Mr. Aidan Carrock might be a fine choice of husband, then she could have her hopes dashed.

"He is unmarried, I believe," she said, slowly. "There is no Mrs. Carrock, but Mr. Aidan appears to manage his affairs very well without a wife."

"When does he arrive?" Judith pursued.

"We have not been given a date. Perhaps Joseph Webb will know. He manages the estate and has been looking after Burroughs this many a month. His wife, Nancy, helps in the house. Would . . . ah . . . would you wish me to discover the precise date for you, Miss Judith?"

Judith heard the careful note in Mrs. Laird's voice. She was showing too much interest in Mr. Aidan Carrock for good manners.

"May I make a suggestion to you, Miss Judith?" Agnes Laird was asking.

Judith's eyes grew a trifle cool. She hated her vulnerable position, yet Mrs.

Laird was intelligent and only made her suggestions when they were likely to be helpful.

"Of course," she said, smoothly.

"Have you considered using Greyfells as a small school? A special school, perhaps? I was thinking, in particular, about children who were, perhaps, not quite so robust as they could be. There was just such a child at the vicar's last parish. He will be eight by now. He was too delicate to go to school, yet he did not do well with a tutor. He needed other children to play with but his mother's health was not good enough for her to have more children. Greyfells is very bracing. A child could benefit from our good mountain air, and you are very well qualified to teach."

Judith had grown thoughtful.

"That is certainly a suggestion worth pondering," she conceded. Her eyes were brighter than they had been for some weeks but Mrs. Laird sighed gently. She suspected that her news about the imminent arrival of Mr.

Carrock had been of more interest to Miss Judith than the suggestion that she should start a school at Greyfells.

A short time later Judith took her leave and walked home with a lighter step, even allowing for the delivery of the box of bric-a-brac for the fête. Mr. Aidan Carrock was coming home, and from all accounts he had not yet found himself a wife. She thought about Bess. She had known for some weeks that the only solution to her problems over Bess was to find her young sister a husband. And who could be more eligible than their wealthy neighbour?

Of course Mr. Aidan Carrock was sure to be informed, shortly after his arrival, that Greyfells had become impoverished . . . there were always people eager to gossip . . . but surely he would not pay too much attention to that after he had set eyes on Bess? She must concentrate on keeping Bess cheered up and looking after her fresh young beauty so that Mr. Carrock could not help but be dazzled by her. It would be perfectly proper for them to call on Mr. Aidan when he arrived home; they were his nearest neighbours. Also, he would already know that Bess's family connections were impeccable; almost as good as his own. She would be extremely suitable as a wife.

And afterwards? Well, afterwards, in order to look after her own interests, she might consider Mrs. Laird's suggestion of turning Greyfells into a school for delicate children. If she could educate a child, and build up his or her small body until that child was fit and strong again, then surely such a school would be a great success. She could charge high fees and would no longer need to worry about money. In her mind's eye she saw a great many small boys running wild on the moorland behind Greyfells, and realised that she was excluding small girls from her plans. But delicate girls were best left to their own parents, thought Judith practically. She would only take children who needed a little extra care. She was not qualified to look after invalids.

Returning home in better spirits, she found that Bess had shut herself in her bedroom and was still sulking. At first Judith decided to coax her out of her ill-temper, then she decided to leave Bess to her own devices for one more day. She was tired, even if she were less anxious than hitherto. Tomorrow she would make a beginning in turning Bess into a future mistress of Burroughs Park.

Tonight she would eat the unappetising meal which Mrs. Armstrong had managed to cook on her last evening at Greyfells and from the housekeeper's looks, Judith felt that she ought to test the food for arsenic! She ate what she could, then retired to her room. After Mrs. Armstrong had gone, she would put her big plan into operation.

Mrs. Armstrong departed next day.

2

BURROUGHS village lay in a hollow about half a mile from Burroughs Park, which was a fine old mansion house built when George I came to the throne. Most of the people living in the village found employment on the Burroughs estate which consisted of a number of farms, rough land for shooting and several stretches of woodland where the deer sheltered and ate the young trees. The more stalwart oak and ash trees were felled for timber required on the estate, and the off-cuts were piled in the log-house for use as fuel.

There was plenty of work for the men and their wives and daughters were pleased to earn a few extra coins in service at the Park, or helping to run the smaller and less ostentatious houses in the neighbourhood.

Judith had little trouble in replacing Mrs. Armstrong with two village women, but she knew she would have to endeavour to train them if Greyfells was going to look attractive enough to meet the eyes of the new owner of Burroughs Park.

Judith had known better than confide her ideas and plans to Bess. If Bess approved a plan, she tended to ruin it by over-eagerness on her part to accomplish her objective, or alternately, she was capable of shutting herself away for days until she looked as though she were going into a decline. Instead Judith had gone up to see her sister in her bedroom and had had no compunction about putting the fear of God into her younger sister.

"You might as well know how we stand," she said, calmly. "Unless we both work together to save Greyfells, we shall be paupers. You wonder why we cannot sell the place and take ourselves off to London. Young Mr. Brent advocates a sale. But if we do so, we shall end up with very little. Father mortgaged it, and if you do not know what *that* means, I shall tell you."

"I do not want to hear!" cried Bess who looked as wet as a sponge.

"But you are going to hear, sister," said Judith. "I am not so very much older than you, and I think we should face our future together. Father borrowed money on the estate. Now it must be paid back or we lose our home. Old Mr. Brent has explained it very well. I intend to help Joss and obtain a profit from our few acres. He can hire a boy to help, young or old so long as he accepts what I can afford to pay. We will grow what we need for ourselves, and sell the surplus."

"But . . . but I *can't* help to grow things!" Bess wailed.

"No, but you can rise from your bed and start to make yourself pretty and help me to receive any visitors who may call. Our mourning period will soon be ended and I want to show everyone that our lives still move forward. You are good with your needle. You must refurbish your gowns and I will try to have one or two new ones made for you."

Bess brightened, though she looked at Judith suspiciously. From her knowledge of her sister, it was more in keeping for Judith to insist that she polished silver and did the flowers.

"Keep your hands pretty," said Judith. "I will use gloves if anyone calls — my hands have roughened a little because of helping Joss. He has to be guided. He will do what I tell him, but I have to learn about the most profitable use of our land. We are like a small postage stamp attached to Burroughs Park, but part of their land was ours at one time. Our great-grandfather sold it to Mr. Aidan Carrock's great-uncle. By the way," she said, casually, "I have heard a whisper that he returns home shortly. We must call on him."

Bess' eyes opened wider with interest,

but she was too young and naïve to be suspicious of her sister's deliberately casual tone when she spoke about Mr. Carrock.

"Oh dear, will it be expected of us?" she asked, nervously.

"Our parents would have made Mr. Aidan Carrock welcome. It is our duty to make him acquainted with his neighbours."

"Yes, I suppose it is," said Bess, rather dismally.

She did not like the sound of their neighbour, having listened to gossip amongst their staff before they were packed off to London. He was, according to rumour, a harsh man and could lash people with his tongue as well as his whip. He had been known to beat one of his servants from his London house before he went abroad on the last occasion. Someone had voiced an opinion that the man had been cruel to Mr. Carrock's favourite dog, but nevertheless Bess shivered. She would keep well clear of Mr. Aidan Carrock, except for that duty visit.

* * *

Judith had set herself a task which was difficult to accomplish on the resources which were at her command. She was managing to run the house, mainly through trial and error and only by using the impending arrival of Mr. Carrock at Burroughs Park as a carrot before the donkey. He would no doubt be a gentleman of taste and culture and she could imagine his raised eyebrows if all was not to his liking.

With that in mind she coaxed and bullied her new servants into keeping the place clean and polished, but twice she had to appeal to young Mr. Brent for an advance on the monies which their investments were earning. This, as was pointed out to her, could not go on.

At the same time, though Joss was

a willing young man, he had little intelligence and once again Judith had to decide on how many hens should be kept as laying hens, and which should be despatched for the pot. Surplus eggs could be sent to the market at Cockermouth, along with fruit and vegetables, but the money earned could not meet the gap between income and expenditure.

Resignedly Judith had to admit to Mrs. Laird that their best hope lay in the school for delicate boys, and Mrs. Laird promised to make a few contacts on her behalf.

Both Bess and Nanny Sherman were loud in their protests against this idea.

"Young hooligans all over the place," Nanny grumbled. "You cannot be serious, Miss Judith."

"I am perfectly serious," said Judith, "and they are not young hooligans. They are delicate boys. We will offer a different kind of school, where their health will be built up as well as their minds."

"Then they will be hooligans if your school is a success," Nanny pointed out.

"I thought you said you had wonderful plans for the future," said Bess, sulkily. "I did not know they would mean having our home invaded."

Judith did not answer for a moment. She had practically given up her idea about marrying off Bess to Mr. Carrock. She had not known that he beat his servants, for whatever reason, when she made those plans and although she sometimes thought that Bess could do with a good spanking, she had no wish to give the task to someone of Mr. Carrock's reputation.

In any case, though rumour had it that Burroughs Park had now been cleaned and refurbished from cellar to attic, there was still no sign of the master's arrival.

"It was not a good idea," she said, sighing. "This one is better. At least we will be well paid for our trouble. I shall want you to help, Nanny, and you too,

Bess. We must get the bedrooms made ready for the boys, and the library will make an excellent classroom."

"Best put away the good ornaments then," said Nanny. "Delicate or not, they are still boys. And, besides, if they really *are* sickly, what happens if they take ill and even die on you, Miss Judith?"

"Do not be silly, Nanny, of course I will not have pupils who are *so* delicate. We must strike a balance. Bess, your hair requires attention. You must not allow your appearance to become careless."

"There is no one to see me here," Bess wailed. "I shall live and die here, an old maid . . . "

"You most certainly will, if you do not take more pains. One never knows who will call after Mr. Aidan Carrock returns home. The countryside is bound to be busier with people travelling a great deal more."

"Oh, bother Mr. Aidan Carrock!" cried Bess, crossly. "He sounds horrible."

Two days later Joss suddenly appeared at the kitchen door, greatly excited, and told them that a large black coach followed by another, full of servants, had arrived at Burroughs Park.

Mr. Aidan Carrock had returned home at last.

3

PRACTICALLY everyone in the neighbourhood attended church the following Sunday, hoping that Mr. Aidan Carrock would arrive and take up the family pew at the front of the church.

Judith had supervised Bess's appearance and for once her sister had no objection to having her hair curled and her cheeks pinched to make them well coloured. Judith, herself, had little time for her own appearance. They were not quite out of mourning and black did not suit her as it did Bess.

In any event, her efforts did not bring more reward than that offered by the usual Sunday sermon from the Reverend Stephen Laird. Mr. Aidan remained firmly closeted at Burroughs Park and had not been known to venture out of doors since his arrival.

Spring was now fully upon them and everywhere fresh yellow daffodils adorned parkland, woodland and cottage garden. Primroses and violets nestled under the hedgerows and the splendid winter shapes of the trees became softened with green as the new leaves were born.

But the mountains, still faintly snow-capped, were full of shadows, pale blue in the mornings shading to deep purple and gold towards sunset. Far out towards the Solway the sun sank low on the horizon, sending out long fingers of rose and silver against a vermilion sky.

Judith loved the colours of her native countryside and often thought that the name of their home, Greyfells, had been ill-chosen. Visitors might find the fells grey and forbidding, but for her they were vibrant with life and colour. The greyness in her spirit was born of this grinding poverty which had been thrust upon her and although the Reverend Stephen Laird taught her that

34

it was the Will of God, Judith could not help feeling that God had been kept extremely busy looking after needy people when he allowed her parents to be taken from them so precipitately.

Impatience had always been her besetting sin, and now she began to feel very impatient with Mr. Carrock. Lying awake at night she had considered the various solutions to her problems, including the delicate boys. The last choice had always been to sell Greyfells and try to find employment of some kind in London, but she was ill-fitted for any sort of commercial undertaking and it would break her heart to part with Greyfells.

The delicate boys was a better idea, but Judith had qualms regarding her handling of such responsibility, in spite of her brave words to Nanny Sherman.

No, by far the best scheme was to marry off Bess to Mr. Aidan Carrock. In fact, it was so perfect that Judith began to believe once more in the Will of God. She had prayed very deeply for forgiveness for her sinful thoughts and perhaps God had listened and was now making amends for the loss of her parents. Mr. Carrock was sure to need a wife, and it would be difficult to find a more eligible husband for Bess.

From listening to gossip of her women helpers from the village, however, Judith gathered that several ladies in the county, who had daughters of marriageable age, were also casting covetous eyes on Burroughs Park. Judith had frowned at this information. She and Bess were Mr. Carrock's nearest neighbours. Why should Mrs. Birkly of Nethergate buy new gowns for her eldest daughter, Lucille, hoping to attract Mr. Carrock? They lived almost sixteen miles from Burroughs Park.

Therefore, Judith argued, if Mr. Carrock chose to hide himself away, it was expedient for her and Bess to call on him and welcome him to the neighbourhood. Surely that was what her mother would have done.

Bess sulked a little when she was

informed that Judith proposed calling on Mr. Carrock the following afternoon at three o'clock. She had built up a mental picture of a great, tall dark ogre of a man and Bess did not think she would be comfortable in his presence.

"He is a personable gentleman," Judith said, impatiently. "Young, wealthy and cultured. Informed, also."

"I thought you had never met him," said Bess, surprised by her sister's knowledge of the man.

"I have not met him," Judith admitted, "but I *assume* he is all of these things. Oh, *do* stop making difficulties, Bess. Do you not see that he is our last hope?"

"For what?"

"A husband, of course," said Judith, recklessly, "for you. Where else are we gong to find anyone suitable before poverty strikes us to the heart and we look shabby beyond anything?"

Bess went pale, and tears rushed to her eyes.

"Oh, no!" she cried, "not *that*,

Judith! He is cruel! He beats his servants."

"They probably deserved to be beaten, and I should like very much to beat you if you do not stop weeping. Your nose will turn pink. Why do you think I have gone to all this trouble to make you look pretty? For Mr. Carrock, of course! Just think what a match it would be! You would have clothes, furs, jewels and all the county would be at your feet. He would be sure to set Greyfells on an even keel, and I would manage very well on our present income . . . or I *think* I would. It could be made to stretch for me, but it is hardly riches for the two of us."

Bess's tears had vanished. A door had been closed in her mind against Mr. Carrock, but Judith's talk of clothes, furs, and jewels had thrown it open widely once more. The only jewellery she owned was a small pearl brooch, bequeathed by her aunt and namesake. It appeared that their mother's jewellery had had to be sold to pay some of their father's debts.

Bess wanted a diamond. Her earliest recollection was of sitting on her mother's knee and pointing a fat finger towards a gold pin, sparkling with diamonds, which ornamented her mother's silk blouse.

"It will be yours one day, my precious," Mrs. Taverner had murmured.

Bess had taken the news that every item of good jewellery must be sold with very bad grace. The diamond pin should have been hers. It had been promised to her all her life and it was exceedingly unfair that it had had to be sold with all the other better pieces of jewellery. Now she only owned the pearl brooch and Judith, a tiny necklace of seed pearls. Agnes Laird had more jewellery than they, and Bess had been most aggrieved about the situation. And, of course, there would also be a ring. If Mr. Carrock offered for her, he would most certainly buy a ring for her.

Bess' eyes were large and solemn at

the thought of acquiring so much of her heart's desire at a stroke. Uneasily she began to remember that she would also acquire Mr. Aidan Carrock with the diamonds. But Judith was very confident that he was a charming, cultured man. If this were really so, then the future began to open up like a flower to the sun. It would be wonderful to be married and have her own establishment instead of continually being forced to do what Judith wished. Her older sister had become very autocratic since she assumed the duties of the head of the family and Bess was becoming rather tired of it.

"What do you wish me to do, Judith?" she asked, humbly, and the elder sister immediately softened.

"Dearest Bess," she said. "I am so glad you see the sense of it. I only want you to look pretty so that Mr. Carrock sees you at your best. And, dearest Bess, please do not think you will be *forced* to marry him if you really feel you cannot. Just remember that the only alternative at the moment is the delicate boys."

Bess shuddered. The thought of having very young males occupying all the spare bedrooms was appalling to her. She was unused to boys and even delicate children could make a great nuisance of themselves. What if Judith's fresh air and exercise only made them even more delicate? What if they all died?

Bess went pale at the thought. Why, Judith might even end up in the hands of the Law . . .

"Will it be all right for me to wear my white gown since we are in mourning until the end of the month?" she asked. "I mean, will not Mr. Carrock expect that I, too, should wear black? Perhaps he will think we ought not to call since we *are* still in mourning, Judith."

Judith tossed her head impatiently. It was the one point which continued to tease her. Was it correct for her to call on Mr. Carrock before their mourning period was finally ended? They were not accepting any social engagements beyond her occasional visit to the Vicarage in order to talk to Mrs. Laird. But at the risk of being thought very bold, she would have to waive convention. How else were they ever going to meet Mr. Carrock? Already she, herself, had worn a lilac gown to church and no eyebrows had been raised. No, it would be quite correct for Bess to wear white if she settled for her old black gown. Bess was very fair whilst she had inherited the dark hair of her father's people. Her own lack of beauty would contrast with her sister's extremely pretty looks.

"We are almost out of mourning," she insisted. "We can both wear lilac now whenever we wish, but you shall wear your white silk. We can pin lilac flowers to the shoulder. You look very well in white, Bess."

Her own looks did not matter in the least.

4

BURROUGHS PARK was a large, imposing Georgian mansion with a fine terraced garden. The many windows had been freshly painted white, and the heavy oak door cleaned and polished.

The door knocker was of heavy brass, fashioned in the shape of a lion's head and Judith banged it imperiously. The butler who opened the door was unknown to her. Old Lomax had retired after Mr. Hugo Carrock died and he now lived in seclusion in a cottage on the estate. The new man was middle-aged with iron-grey hair and a long nose. Judith received the impression that he was looking at them down that nose, and for a moment she was filled with qualms. How could she have put herself and Bess in a position of such indignity!

She drew a deep breath and reminded herself that she was Miss Taverner of Greyfells, then announced herself as such to the butler.

"Miss Taverner and Miss Elizabeth of Greyfells," she said, clearly. "We have called to see Mr. Aidan Carrock."

The man bowed and conducted them to the entrance hall, asking them to be seated whilst he informed his master. The hall had changed in some subtle fashion since Mr. Hugo's day, thought Judith, looking round. Yet it was difficult to appreciate precisely where the difference lay. Portraits hung on the walls and the elegant tables, chairs and sofas remained the same. But the floor had been polished to mirror brightness, then covered with beautiful Oriental rugs, and Judith began to appreciate what had happened. Everything sparkled with cleanliness. Mrs. Hugo Carrock had allowed her servants to grow lax and the odour of many dogs had tended to pervade Burroughs Park.

Now Judith's nose wrinkled. Very faintly she could detect the fragrance of perfume. Perfume! Yet Mrs. Laird had stated that Mr. Carrock had no female relatives, and it was unlikely that a maidservant should use perfume. She turned to Bess whose eyes had grown enormous with apprehension and whose cheeks had lost all colour despite repeated pinchings, intending to ask if she, too, could detect the fragrance.

"I do not feel well," Bess whispered.

"It is too late for that now," Judith hissed. "Take hold of yourself, sister."

The butler, who was surely a personage in his own right, returned to the hall and asked the young ladies to follow him. A moment later they were shown into the large drawing room where a fire burned brightly in the hearth. Almost straight away Judith was once again struck by the new look of the room. The chintz chair covers had been laundered to perfection, the floors and furniture polished mirror-bright, and the Aubusson carpet cleaned until it looked like new. Judith, however, recognised the very distinctive pattern.

Once again the faint fragrance of delicate perfume lingered in the air, but there was nothing of the fop in the gentleman who came forward to greet them. He had been sitting at a writing desk in the corner of the room and from the window he must have been able to see the arrival of his two visitors. He wore a well-cut coat and trousers in fine black woolcloth, but his white shirt was immaculate and of the finest silk. His hair was very black and his skin darkened by exposure to the sun so that at first glance his appearance was quite foreign. His piercing black eyes surveyed both young ladies and if Bess could have found a way of escape, she would have taken it. Mr. Aidan Carrock bore out all her worst fears.

Then suddenly he smiled and held out his hand. On his small finger he wore a heavy gold ring, in the centre of which sparkled a beautiful diamond of the first water. Bess almost gasped aloud when she saw it, and she even managed a smile for Mr. Carrock.

"Ah, Miss Taverner," he bowed, turning gracefully to Judith then to Bess, "and Miss Elizabeth. How very thoughtful of you both to call and bid me welcome to the neighbourhood."

His face sobered and for a moment he looked quiet and considerate.

"Allow me to express my condolences at the loss of your parents. I am only newly acquainted with the affairs of my neighbours, and there are matters which I may wish to discuss with you, Miss Taverner, at a later date but meantime we will partake of refreshment."

The butler had carried in a silver tray bearing a decanter of wine, crystal glasses and a plate of ratafia biscuits.

"May I offer you a glass of Madeira, Miss Taverner? Miss Elizabeth?"

"We prefer to drink tea," said Judith.

"The wine will revive you after your walk from Greyfells."

He poured two small glasses and

offered the biscuits which both ladies declined. He smiled a little and asked the butler to bring tea.

"I must say that it pleases me very much to have come to live in such a sociable area," he said, easily, and the light was back in his eyes as though they were filled with laughter. "Several of my neighbours have already called and I have made the acquaintance of quite a few young ladies. It is indeed a great pleasure to one who has lived abroad for so many years to be made so welcome on my return."

Judith began to flush. So they were not the first! It was evident that Mr. Carrock had already been pursued by a number of ladies with eligible daughters, and that he was well aware of their interest in him.

"And you, Miss Elizabeth, what do you like to do with your time? . . . when you are not in mourning, of course. Do you ride?"

"But of course, everyone rides here, sir," Judith said, swiftly. In fact, Bess was afraid of horses and had been a constant irritation to her father because of it. "Unfortunately we have preferred to live very quietly since . . . since the death of our parents." She was chagrined to hear her own voice faltering a little.

"My sympathies, Miss Taverner," he again assured her, gravely.

"Bess can sew and paint, and she sings and plays the piano very well."

Bess opened her mouth to protest that she was barely adequate at any of these skills, but Judith was giving her warning looks and she knew when to hold her tongue.

Mr. Carrock was listening to Judith with marked attention, his eyes scarcely leaving her face and Bess suddenly saw her sister as Mr. Carrock must do, and her cheeks reddened a little with embarrassment. Judith was always careful to be well enough groomed. Her hair was normally neat and she was clean about her person, but her black gown was very drab and her shoes well worn with all the walking which they were now required to do. Her hair was luxuriant and curled much more riotously than Bess' own fair hair, but Judith had tried to bring it under control with hair pins and combs. However, the spring breezes had been capricious and now it escaped in small tendrils of curls which fell about her forehead and behind her ears.

She had unusual looks with slightly high cheek bones and slanting eyes of a deep sapphire blue. A few particles of dust had been brushed impatiently from her right cheek and had formed themselves into a long streak of dirt. If only Judith would take as much interest in her own appearance as she took in hers, thought Bess, then there would be no need for embarrassment. Not that she would be likely to catch a husband! But it did not help one's own prospects to be introduced to a possible suitor by a sister so careless about making the best of her own appearance.

"Bess also makes excellent sweet-meats," Judith soldiered on, even though she had the strangest feeling that Mr. Aidan Carrock's absorbed interest was all a sham and he had heard just such a recital several times before. He was listening very carefully, however, and nodding slightly as he turned to look at Bess. Once again there was a smile on his face and his eyes seemed to dance with golden lights.

Suddenly the French windows opened and a young woman, older than Judith but with all the gaiety and high spirits of youth, almost danced into the room.

"*Est-ce que je vous dérange?*" she asked.

Mr. Carrock rose to his feet and greeted the newcomer in voluble French, taking both her small hands in his and kissing her fingers.

"Allow me to present Mrs. Carrock," he said, formally, drawing the girl forward to meet Judith, then Elizabeth.

"*Françoise, chérie, permettez-moi*

de vous présenter à Mlle. Taverner et Mlle. Elizabeth Taverner."

Judith had thought that her own looks were dark, but this girl's long hair was raven black and her eyes sparkled like black diamonds. Her skin was the warm rich hue of apricots and the sweet delicate perfume which she had already noticed was now very fragrant in her nostrils.

"Mrs. Carrock speaks little English. She is from Martinique."

Judith's face had flushed scarlet, then the colour receded, leaving her very white.

"I am sure you must be very busy, Madame," she said, quietly. "We . . . my sister and I . . . "

Mrs. Carrock began to answer in French, but Mr. Carrock held up a slender hand and spoke to her rapidly. She stopped swinging her skirts and stood beside him, her eyes downcast.

"We will trouble you no further," Judith went on. "It has been quite an . . . an education to meet you,

Mr. Carrock, and . . . of course . . . "
she turned to the dark girl, " . . . *Mrs.*
Carrock. We are not yet entertaining at
Greyfells . . . "

"Nevertheless, I would like to have
the privilege of calling upon you in a
business capacity," said Mr. Carrock,
swiftly.

Judith inclined her head very slightly.
She had no wish to have anything
further to do with Aidan Carrock,
but her rather well-developed sense of
curiosity was at war with her feelings
of propriety. What business could he
possibly wish to discuss with her? She
could think of nothing which they
could have in common.

She could hear the French girl's
warm rich voice very clearly as the
butler conducted her and Bess to
the front door. She had assured
Mr. Carrock that the short walk to
Greyfells would be an enjoyment to
both her and Bess, but the ground
seemed very hard on their feet as they
walked home, and Bess would like to

have dissolved into tears but for the fact that Judith had gone into one of her black moods. That meant that she was very angry about something; too angry even to talk about it.

Bess almost ran ahead of her as they took the long winding path through the woods which led to the gravelled drive in front of Greyfells. It was little more than an elegant farm-house compared with Burroughs Park, but Bess had not realised, until now, how much she loved the place.

She stopped outside their own front door and waited for Judith. Now that the question had been resolved for them and she would not have to contemplate marriage with Mr. Carrock, Bess felt considerably more cheerful. She still wanted a diamond, but the cost might have been too high if she had been obliged to marry that man. His French wife was very high-spirited now, but she might be less full of '*joie de vivre*' in a few years time!

"I am not disappointed, Judith, truly

I am not," she declared to Judith. "I did not like Mr. Carrock."

"He is a scoundrel," said Judith, furiously. "How dare he!"

"But . . . but I was not *promised* to him, Judith. I mean, we did not know he had a wife."

Judith looked as though she would explode. How she hated to be crossed, thought Bess. She always liked to have her own way. How she wished that someone young and kind would offer for her, and that she could have her own establishment, well away from Judith's tantrums. She was afraid of what her sister would do next, and of how she intended to arrange Bess's life for her.

"I am going to my room, Judith," said Bess. "My feet hurt."

"Oh, very well. You can cry as much as you wish. It does not matter now."

Bess nodded. Already the tears were not far away.

5

JUDITH had decided that she had seldom met anyone she disliked more. Mr. Carrock had intimated that he intended to call upon her by way of business. Well, he would not find her a very amenable business associate. She had nothing to say to him. Instead she lost no time in visiting Mrs. Laird once more and asking her if anything could be arranged with regard to the delicate boys.

"I have already contacted two families," Mrs. Laird confessed, "with tentative enquiries on your behalf. I explained that you may or may not wish to go ahead with the project, but a short note would be sufficient for the parents to oversee your accommodation, and what you offer by way of education. They would be happy to travel to Greyfells as soon as is convenient."

"I will set the maids to clean the bedrooms and to make them suitable for children. We will require to air the bed linen," said Judith, practically. "The library can soon be rearranged as a schoolroom and I shall find pencils and papers for my pupils. My father had more than enough of both. I am most grateful to you, Mrs. Laird, for this idea which you put forward. I am doubtful about fees, however. What sum of money ought I to charge?"

The Reverend Stephen Laird had been brought into the discussion on this point and a figure was calculated to the satisfaction of all three.

"I cannot take more than six boys at any one time, for the moment," said Judith.

"You would acquire three from the two families I mentioned," said Mrs. Laird, "a boy of eight and twin boys of seven. The twins have been delicate since birth, and Matthew, the other boy, has not recovered well from a bad winter cold. He has loss of appetite."

"I shall set Nanny Sherman to making something to tempt his appetite, and Bess will be required to help." Her young face hardened. "I think they each understand that it is essential. Perhaps my experiment should not include more than these three boys in the beginning."

"If you feel that it is going to be successful, I will enquire further on your behalf," Mrs. Laird promised.

★ ★ ★

Mr. and Mrs. Arnold Dickson and Mrs. Lydia Forsyth called to inspect Greyfells two weeks later, and Judith agreed to take Matthew Dickson and Peter and Sam Forsyth for a trial period commencing mid-May until the end of June. If this was of benefit to the boys, then further arrangements could be made. Both families were native to Manchester.

Nanny Sherman disapproved strongly of the new venture and low murmurings of foreboding could be heard as she walked about with a long face and downcast eyes. Her sulky temper acted perversely on the other housemaids who had settled into Greyfells very happily under Judith's stronger management, and they had prepared the spare rooms with energy and enthusiasm for the new arrivals.

Bess, too, had brightened. Something new was happening and her boredom was relieved. She was confident that she could teach the boys painting and singing whilst Judith attended to the basic subjects, but once every day Judith proposed taking them for a walk over the rough ground which her father had used as a breeding ground for game, to the higher craggy ground which bordered Burroughs Park. This would strengthen their limbs, fill their lungs with fresh air and improve their appetites for their evening meal which would consist of good plain food cooked by Nanny Sherman.

"At least you can do *that*, Nanny," said Judith. "You did it most successfully for my sister and myself, as I remember."

"I don't know what dear Mrs. Taverner would say," said Nanny, with a great deal of head shaking.

"If she were here to say it, there would be no need to educate and build up delicate boys," said Judith, rather cruelly. "You will have to help, Nanny, or . . . or . . . " She left the words unfinished.

"I never thought to see the day, Miss Judith," Nanny quavered. "You've grown into a very hard young woman. It does not become you at all. It is not becoming to any young lady to be so hard."

"Circumstances force me to be hard, Nanny," said Judith, grimly. "It is not the worst fault, I am quite sure."

She thought about Mr. Carrock and her lips tightened. How glad she was that her plans had gone awry. She would not have wished to see Bess married to such a man.

Mr. Carrock had been absent from Burroughs Park, having gone to London on business, but a few days before the boys were due to arrive at Greyfells, he called and enquired for Miss Taverner.

Nanny Sherman had gone to open the door in answer to the peal of bells which sounded in the kitchen, and her eyes peered at him with interest as she asked him to wait in the entrance hall and went to find Judith who was unpacking a few teaching books which she had been obliged to purchase.

"*Who* is it, Nanny?" she asked, after Nanny had mumbled a name.

"The new gentleman from Burroughs Park, Miss Judith. Mr. Aidan Carrock."

Judith's face began to flush and her blue eyes sparked fire.

"Ah! So Mr. Carrock gives me the honour of a call," she said, bitingly. "I will see him in the small study, Nanny . . . my father's small business room."

"There is no fire, Miss Judith, and

it is a dull day. We'll not see the real warmth until the end of the month."

"No, it is not particularly comfortable," Judith agreed. "It is a splendid place to discuss business with our neighbour, Nanny. Oh, and if Miss Bess is about, please tell her she is not obliged to be sociable. There is no need for her presence, Nanny."

"He seems a fine set-up man, Miss Judith. I would have thought you would want to make more fuss."

"We are not always what we seem, Nanny," said Judith, darkly.

The old woman conducted Mr. Aidan Carrock to the rather cold and cheerless study which John Taverner had used as his den. It had been little used since then and as a result it had become a trifle dusty and neglected.

When Judith arrived she found Mr. Carrock looking round distastefully She was now out of heavy mourning and wore a simple checked lavender gown with creamy lace at the neck and wrists. Its freshness suited her and anger had lent colour and sparkle to her face so that for a moment Mr. Carrock's black eyes surveyed her with frank interest, and golden lights began to dance in his eyes.

"It is good of you to see me, Miss Taverner," he said, formally.

She inclined her head, hoping to indicate that she was in full agreement.

"Please sit down, Mr. Carrock. Unfortunately we are not so well served as you are at Burroughs Park, but Nanny Sherman will presently bring tea and honeycake."

"I need little refreshment, ma'am," said Mr. Carrock, politely.

His eyes once again flickered round the room, and following his gaze, Judith began to regret that she had not asked Nanny to show Mr. Carrock into the drawing room. But embarrassment only lent fuel to the fire of her anger against him.

"You wished to see me," she prompted, "on business, I understand?"

"Indeed, yes. With your permission I would like us to scrutinize a map of our adjoining lands, with special reference to one particular field. At present you own this field, Miss Taverner, but I would be happy to offer a very reasonable sum if you would consider selling it to me. It is this field of rough ground which leads to this high ground on my property."

Judith recognised the field immediately. She planned to use the field so that her delicate boys would have the maximum amount of exercise. It was rough, but not too rough for growing boys, and it housed a great deal of wild life which would benefit their education.

Recently a yellow pine marten had been seen in the vicinity and had accounted for some of the game. Had Mr. Carrock proved to be a different type of gentleman, Judith might have asked him to despatch the marten since Joss was certain that it had accounted for a few lambs and even one sheep, being of unusual size and strength. It had been spotted crawling, snake-like, along ledges on high ground belonging to Burroughs Park, and Judith had no qualms about desiring to see the last of it.

But Mr. Carrock had quite enough land, including land which had originally been owned by Greyfells, to be allowed to purchase more. She had her own requirements to consider.

"I would not dream of selling . . . " quickly he named a price, " . . . my land," she ended a trifle less stridently. "Burroughs Park has already benefited too much from the misfortunes of Greyfells."

"Mismanagement," he corrected, his face hardening. Again his eyes swept round the shabby room. "I would not come to you but for the fact that I need the land badly, otherwise a project of mine could be jeopardized . . . "

"I cannot imagine how my land could help or hinder any of your projects," she interrupted, "and I have no interest in listening to some lengthy

65

explanation, sir. The land is not for sale."

He pursed his lips, then repeated his offer, increasing it substantially.

"You must know the price of land, Miss Taverner," he said, coolly. "My offer far exceeds the normal price."

She swallowed. The money would be a Godsend to her at the moment. Her father's solicitors were required, every month, to pay back the mortgage which her father had taken out. It was paid into a bank in Carlisle, and no doubt transferred to the finance company which, it appeared, would hold the mortgage for the next seven years. Seven years seemed a lifetime to Judith.

"Come now, Miss Taverner," Mr. Carrock said, impatiently. "I know that finances are not good for you or your sister. I know very well how you are placed."

Again the colour mounted her cheeks.

"I have no idea why you should be so concerned about my affairs," she said, angrily. "I have said I will not sell, Mr. Carrock. I mean every word of it." She paused, then smiled, her eyes gleaming.

"I notice that you have not brought your . . . ah . . . young lady to call."

"Young lady?"

"The French lady. *Je vous demande pardon* . . . Madame Carrock."

Her French accent was perfect and she had the satisfaction of seeing him disconcerted.

"So you understood?"

"Every word. And enough to know that she is *not* your wife. You were merely using her to be rid of ambitious women with marriageable daughters . . . and sisters! . . . on their hands."

"I notice that you brought along Miss Elizabeth as a possible attraction, but did not offer yourself in the same capacity." His eyes were once again gleaming with amusement, and after her initial broadsides, he had once more gained complete control of the situation.

"I have no wish to find a husband for myself. I can arrange my life very well as it is."

Again he grinned and her fury grew.

"Mlle. Françoise asked if she had done well. I wonder what you told her, sir? That she did *very* well? But she did not fool me. I could see straight away that she was not your wife, but merely your whore."

She was unprepared for the fury which lit up his eyes.

"How *dare* you, Miss Taverner!" he said in a low, controlled voice. "I cannot believe that your mother would be proud to hear you making such a remark. I . . . I have it in mind to ask your nice old Nanny Sherman to wash out your mouth with soap. Do not let me hear such a word on a lady's lips again, or I shall be obliged to . . . to spank you."

Her face was very pale and she had caught her lip between her teeth. Bitterly she was regretting her forward remarks. It should not matter to her whether Mr. Carrock kept a wife *or* a mistress at Burroughs Park.

"I . . . I apologise," she croaked.

"So you should, and the young lady should also have your apology. She is the daughter of an old friend from Martinique and her father has recently died. She and her mother are both living at Burroughs Park, though Madame de Ridieux is indisposed. They have a coloured servant who cares for them."

"I . . . I see," she said, weakly. "I . . . I am truly sorry."

"She is also . . ."

"No . . . please!" she interrupted, quickly. "It was unforgivable of me, and there is no need to explain further."

"As you wish. We will say no more about it. No doubt, since your French is so good, you will enjoy making friends with my guests."

His voice had grown unexpectedly kind and gentle.

"Think about my offer, Miss Judith. It is not a bad one, and you would still have enough land around Greyfells for you to manage."

The gentle tones were disturbing to her emotionally, much more so than his anger or contempt. She wanted to put her hands over her face and allow the tears to flow, then her anger began to stir again. Was not this very gentleness always much more effective when trying to gain one's ends? Mr. Carrock was merely trying to ingratiate himself with her so that she would agree to sell her land.

"I told you that I do not intend to sell any more land," she said, flatly.

"Not even to meet your mortgage?"

She flushed. "You are very well informed about my affairs, Mr. Carrock. I suppose your spies will also have informed you as to the extent of the mortgage and how it is met. I suppose you know the exact sum which our solicitors allow us every month for the expenses of Greyfells. Well, sir, perhaps you do *not* know everything."

His eyes regarded her gravely, then

they lit up once more with amusement.

"Perhaps I do not. I will not take up more of your time, Miss Taverner."

He took her hand. "Nevertheless, neighbours are required to help one another in troubled times. Do not hesitate to call upon me should you require assistance at any time."

"I have become used to managing my own affairs, sir."

She had forgotten to wear her gloves and he turned her hand over, noting the slender and delicate shape of her fingers and how the soft skin had become roughened and calloused with the work she had to do. She had tried to pull her hands away, but he held her fingers tightly, then let her go.

"I will not detain you, sir," she said, putting her hands behind her back. "You must be kept busy with the affairs of your estate since you apparently have a great many projects on hand."

"I see that you, too, are busy, Miss Taverner. There is no need to see me out. I know the way. Thank you for giving me your time, ma'am, however unprofitable for me."

Curiosity gnawed at her. She longed to know why he wanted the rough field, but she would have died rather than ask. She could imagine his feigned astonishment at such curiosity on her part.

"My respects to Miss Elizabeth."

He walked out swiftly, and she sat down to control her trembling knees. She had been so sure that the French girl was a . . . a lightskirt he had brought home in order that he would be relieved of the attentions of match-making women. And she had called Mlle. Françoise an unpardonable name! Perhaps the young lady was his fiancée. She had suspected that he was going to inform her of this when she stopped him. She did not want to hear his confidences. At least . . . it might have been interesting to know, had she not been feeling so stiff-necked. In any case, nothing had changed. She would never allow Bess to become bound to such a man in marriage. He would treat her like a rag doll to be thrown about as his fancy took him, and without the ability to answer back. Bess was much too soft for Mr. Carrock.

Judith sighed deeply, feeling tired and dispirited after expending so much energy on anger. How dare he investigate her private affairs so thoroughly! He had no doubt done so in order to assess how much he would be obliged to offer for the field. If only she could acquire a really good income from her school for delicate boys, how wonderful it would be. In the dark hours of the night she had secretly viewed the prospect with misgiving, but it was the best she could do, and she was grateful to Mrs. Agnes Laird for her help.

She sighed again. There was no doubt that she could be in a worse position. At least she and Bess had a home, and food. She would count her blessings.

6

JUDITH had decided that her blessings numbered three; Matthew Dickson, Peter Forsyth and Sam Forsyth. The twins were identical and Judith decided that she would have difficulty in distinguishing one from the other, but after only a few days Peter emerged as a fairly dynamic boy for one so delicate. Sam would require a great deal more care and attention.

Matthew Dickson was pale-faced and tall for his age. He wheezed a little and Judith could see that he did, indeed, require to be built up physically. His parents had been rather fussy and perhaps a trifle disparaging about his accommodation at Greyfells, deciding that the furnishings of his bedroom were not exactly new.

"They have been well cleaned," Judith defended. "Surely they are adequate for a child."

"Of course they are, Arnold," Mrs. Dickson had said when her husband would have demurred. "They will be splendid for Matthew. Do not be so nit-picking, Arnold," she had muttered to her husband under her breath. "You know I need a rest away from Matthew now. He is forever whining round my skirts."

Judith had pretended not to hear. Now she surveyed Matthew closely. Would he also want to whine around *her* skirts?

Mrs. Forsyth, on the other hand, had approved of everything. She had a needle-sharp voice and an extremely lady-like appearance. Her husband, James, sold cotton cloth and was a successful business man. Mr. Dickson, on the other hand, was in the tobacco trade. Judith professed ignorance of both trades, hardly thinking it was relevant to the education of the boys. She would teach them basic subjects and they would no doubt be sent to good schools as soon as their strength and energy were up to a more robust education.

Nanny still grumbled for two days, but with less and less vigour as she began to look after the boys.

"Poor lambs," she said to Judith, "a puff o' wind would blow that Sam away."

"They have been delicate since they were born," said Judith. "Twins, you know."

"Poor lambs," said Nanny, again, "and that Matthew! He won't be long for this world," she added, dolefully.

"Oh, Nanny! *Don't* say that," cried Judith. "He has only had a cold."

"His tubes," said Nanny. "You should listen to his tubes. That's where it tells."

"Well, just see to it that we nourish them up . . . the boys, I mean."

"Soups . . . good rich game, trout and salmon. Nothing fancy. Lamb, maybe and honey pudding with creamy milk fresh from the cow. Nothing fancy, like in the town."

"I leave that in your capable hands, Nanny."

"I did not realise they were such poor creatures, Miss Judith. And you cramming their heads with learning. Oh, but Greyfells is a strange place these days."

Strange and frightening! Judith made sure that her three small charges were comfortable, and warned them against what they must or must not do in the house. They surveyed their new classroom with solemn eyes, and weighed up one another with speculation whilst Judith eyed all three nervously. Suppose she could not handle them sufficiently well to please their parents. The thought made her feel very young and insecure.

Matthew Dickson decided that he could soon lick Sam Forsyth into shape, and Peter, too . . . but perhaps not quite so easily. Otherwise the place was strange and rather frightening for him, too. There were no streets, and no carriages continually on the move. There were few people walking across the fells, with the possible exception of the shepherds and their dogs and, worst of all, there were no shops or stores where one could buy sweetmeats or model soldiers. He was going to be a soldier when he grew up. His mother had promised that he would not go into Trade, like his father. His mother had been born a lady, but had fallen on hard times. She said Miss Taverner was also a lady, but she was only a teacher, in Matthew's book, and he would wait to see whether or not he liked her.

Peter Forsyth had already made up his mind. He hated that boy with the wheezing voice and the snivel behind his nose. That boy intended to fight him, and Peter gave this due consideration and wondered whether or not he would win. It was a great grief to him that he and Sam were so small for their age.

Their mother had claimed that Miss Taverner would help them to grow up big and strong, but Peter had tried not to scoff aloud. How could a female teacher help one to grow strong? She was no different from some of the governesses who had tried to teach him and Sam. They had soon given up when they found it was not so easy as they had imagined. Like Matthew, he viewed the wide landscape with misgiving. He had been forced to come and Peter hated to be forced to do anything against his will, therefore he had decided to run away if he did not like Greyfells.

The terrain was daunting, though, and Miss Taverner had promised them a good view of the wildlife around Greyfells, especially amongst the crags. There were foxes and badgers, eagles and buzzards. There would be rabbits and hares, stoats and weasels, and Peter had listened with widened eyes, as his new teacher described all these creatures. They were wild creatures, unlike the old dogs and fat cats which wandered freely about the place. They were even more wild than the farmyard animals, especially the geese and the few turkeys. The wild creatures were used to killing for food. They may be shy of men, tall and strong, with a gun at their shoulder, but suppose they were confronted by a small boy, perhaps their sharp, cruel teeth would sink into his flesh and the pain would be excruciating. Peter shivered at the thought. He felt that he was a prisoner in this old house and he was not at all happy at the thought.

Sam had his own feelings about Greyfells. Being so small and delicate, he had never sought to be competitive, and had coaxed his father to buy him books instead of the obligatory soldiers, sailing boats and ball games suitable for a growing boy. Through his books he had learned to love the countryside. Greyfells was, indeed, the lonely house in the woods of 'Once upon a time'. and Miss Taverner was the beautiful princess.

Miss Elizabeth was also beautiful,

but her mouth became cross at times, just like his mother's. The cows, sheep, young lambs, hens, ducks and even the bad-tempered geese and turkeys were all familiar to him, and it seemed to him that he was living in a fairy-tale which had come true. He loved the beautiful shapes of the mountains, the colours, the movement of the shadows caused by the sun and the brightness of the moon and stars when it was time for him to go to sleep and he slipped back out of bed and hooked back the window shutters.

Sam had never been so happy. Not even Matthew could dampen his deep inner contentment. He had been educated with other boys once before when his mother decided to try a small preparatory school for him and Peter. It had not been a success. The boys had been rather rough and he and Peter had copied a few phrases and sayings which had shocked their parents. On the whole, however, the other boys had left them alone. He could put up with Matthew quite well.

★ ★ ★

Judith decided to give the boys a few days in which to settle into Greyfells before starting lessons seriously. She felt that they all had to get to know one another and to take one another on trust. She was encouraging Bess to help by inventing games, because the weather, always capricious, had settled for rain and large black storm clouds swept in from the Solway and lashed the windows with rain.

No appetites were developed because of all this inactivity and Nanny's good, plain food was not enjoyed. She shook her head when a few slices of pheasant were left on a plate and her treacle tart with cream not quite eaten up.

"I hope you boys are not going to be pernickety," she said, severely. "I serve up good plain food and I expect you to eat it."

They stared back at her unhappily wondering how to explain that it was more than they could manage.

"A young lady has called to see you, Miss Judith," Nanny announced in the afternoon. "I have shown her into the drawing room."

"Who is it this time?" Judith asked.

She suspected that news that she had started teaching had reached the ears of those neighbours who might look down their noses. Already people had started to call, but a few had hinted broadly that it was not quite the thing, and as the days passed, Judith noted that fewer people were calling than her parents had entertained. She had clearly heard Mrs. Ashton-Brown referring to her as 'poor Judith Taverner' in church the previous Sunday.

"She says her name is Mrs. Carrock," said Nanny, with no little astonishment. "I did not know Mr. Aidan Carrock had married a black woman."

"She is not a black woman," said Judith, "besides . . . "

Besides, they were apparently determined to keep up the myth that Mlle. Françoise de Ridieux was Aidan Carrock's wife! Judith thought that they might have done her the honour of being truthful with *her*, at least, now that she knew this was all pretence.

Rather haughtily she left Bess and the boys to pursue a guessing game, and walked to the drawing room where Joss Peters had filled the log basket and added a few logs to the fire. Now it burned brightly and Mlle. Françoise looked round appreciatively.

"Ah, how cosee," she said, haltingly. "My dear Aidan, he tell me you speak my language, but I mus' learn to speak with yours. It ees ver' good, no?"

"No . . . yes!" said Judith. "Yes, if you wish."

"Your home ees so leetle, so nice. I was bored and Maman fretful. So I come. The rain, he will not melt me down, no?"

"No." Despite her disapproval of Françoise's pretences, Judith could not suppress a smile. The French girl was very beautiful. Mr. Carrock must surely wish to marry her. If she had not heard Françoise asking him if she had acted the part of his wife very well, she would have supposed them already married.

"Nanny Sherman will dry your cloak, Mlle. Françoise," she said, "and your carriage and the horses will be attended to by Joss. Would you care for tea, or would you prefer wine?"

"I like the wine," said Françoise frankly. "Dearest Aidan say it made me twirl in the head. I like too much of it."

"One small glass, then, Mademoiselle," said Judith.

"Ah non . . . *not* mademoiselle . . . Madame! But you may call me Françoise. See I wear the wedding ring *this* hand." She held out her right hand.

Judith's mouth fell open.

"You mean . . . you *are* married to Mr. Aidan Carrock, after all?"

"I marry his brother, mon mari,

Simon. I am Madame . . . non, non,
. . . I am *Mrs.* Simon Carrock. Simon
comes with us from Martinique, but he
has business in London for government
affairs. He was government officer in
Dominica, but we meet when he come
to Martinique, and we marry. But my
papa is dead and we bring Maman for
holiday, and she is seeck. Dear Aidan
say we come to Burroughs Park until
Simon ready to return to Martinique
and Dominica. Then we go home with
Maman and Chloe. She look after
Maman and me, like your old one."

"Nanny Sherman."

"Truly."

Judith bit her lip. "And truly I
must apologise to you, Mrs. Carrock
. . . Françoise . . . I am deeply ashamed
of misunderstanding."

"I know. You thought me French
whore," said Françoise, happily. "Very
funny."

Judith's face had gone very red.

"I . . . I don't know what to say."

"I laugh. Maman, she is ver' strict,

86

as was Papa. But I think French whore would be fun, no?"

"No!" cried Judith. "Do not *say* so at Burroughs Park. *Please*, Madame Françoise . . . I . . . really am ashamed."

"I tell Simon, that is all," said Françoise. "If Aidan does not marry and I make baby with Simon, he is heir to Burroughs Park, so we are important there."

"Oh. I . . . I see," said Judith, somewhat stupidly. She had never met anyone quite like Françoise before. She did not think the French girl ought to be so frank about her personal affairs.

"He is ver' good catch," said Françoise, happily, "if you desire a good husband."

"Well, I do not," said Judith, crossly. "I have started a school for delicate boys. I can earn my own living here at Greyfells, without having to consider marrying anyone."

Françoise looked at her curiously. "And you like to teach other people's sons, instead of making your own?"

"It is not like that!"

"Perhaps Aidan will be too slow to offer for you. Would you like me to give him the prod?"

"No!" cried Judith, again. She was beginning to feel exhausted. How *did* one deal with Françoise? Her eyes were wide with innocence, but for a moment Judith suspected that there was mischief in their depths. Was the French girl playing with her?

She shook her head. "I could not marry without love, Françoise."

"Ah ... love. Soon you would love Aidan. I love Aidan. He is ver' lovable."

"I think the rain has now cleared," said Judith, staring pointedly out of the window. "Perhaps it would be wise for you to travel back to Burroughs Park before the clouds gather once again."

Françoise heaved a great sigh as she stood up.

"Ah, I understand. You show me the door."

Judith flushed. "I . . . I do not wish you to get wet," she said, lamely.

"Already I have the wet, but I go now. Soon I shall see you again. Perhaps we will be friends."

She lapsed into French and Judith responded almost automatically.

"You have lived in France?" asked Françoise, as she walked towards the door.

"No, but my teacher was a French lady from Paris. I have a good ear for sounds and we talked a great deal. For one day a week everyone spoke French at my school. I liked learning the language, but my sister did not. She does not speak it very well."

"She is ver' pretty. She will marry soon, I theenk."

Judith watched her go, hardly knowing how she felt about Mrs. Françoise Carrock. She would reserve judgement, she decided, trying to look on the visit sensibly, but underneath she liked the French girl. Secretly, too, she was pleased that Mr. Aidan Carrock was her brother-in-law and not her fiancé, though why that should matter to her, she had no idea at all. His affairs were no concern of hers.

7

TWO days later Judith settled down to the hard work of trying to teach three small boys, two of whom had little interest in learning. She had one more visitor in the welcome shape of Mrs. Agnes Laird, who had approved whole-heartedly her arrangements at Greyfells and dismissed one or two disturbances as 'teething troubles'. Sam had been feeling sick and Judith had decided that the food might be rather rich for him. Less of Nanny's 'good plain fare' might be more beneficial. Nanny had gone into a huff for a little while, but had decided to give the boys freshly baked bread and her own home-made strawberry jam for tea, but without the accompanying bowl of rich cream. Perhaps that would have to be added to the menu gradually. The poor lambs had been underfed for too long.

"Cumberland herb pudding," said Mrs. Laird, "now that should put them right! I shall remind Nanny Sherman."

Judith made a face. "I do not like it. You will remind Nanny so that she will insist that we all eat her herb pudding, just when I have trained her to forget all about it."

"No sacrifice is too great, Miss Judith," said Mrs. Laird.

"Very true," Judith sighed. "Cumberland herb pudding it is then."

She thought about the concoction which combined wild plants such as freshly-picked dandelion and nettle leaves with barley, the whole being steamed in a pudding basin to preserve all the goodness. Once a year it was served in springtime in order to clear the blood of winter impurities.

"I hope it does not encourage Matthew to become too energetic again and to fight Peter Forsyth once more. Both boys are very proud of their bruises and scratches, and we have all of us considered that honour has been served on all sides."

"I am quite sure that it has," said Mrs. Laird, comfortably. "I saw the boys racing about the garden as I walked here. I am sure their health is better already. It is so pleasant that the weather is fine again. Mr. Carrock has once again travelled to London, I believe. He apparently has many business interests, including sugar in the West Indies."

"His sister-in-law did not accompany him, I suppose?"

"I do not know," said Mrs. Laird. "We hear little about her. You see, she is Catholic," she added by way of explanation. "But Mr. Laird has met Mr. Simon Carrock and found him a very quiet, rather distinguished gentleman. Having now met Mrs. Carrock, I find her an . . . an *unusual* choice of wife for him. And she behaves in a rather forward fashion to Mr. Aidan Carrock, himself. Her mother is still indisposed, or so I understand."

Judith looked at Mrs. Laird and smiled. She had always thought Agnes Laird the most perfect woman, to be admired and even copied for good behaviour. But now that she, herself, was head of a household and more used to dealing first hand with people, she could see that Mrs. Laird was quite human after all. She was piqued because she had not known about Françoise. Now she tended to criticize her a little. Yet Judith could hardly blame her. If the Reverend Stephen Laird and his wife had been treated to the same frankness as she had received from Françoise, then they would assuredly look askance at her!

* * *

Judith had been afraid that she had no gift for teaching. She had found it very difficult to train her village maidservants into good service in the house and had tired herself out keeping an eagle eye on them in case they ignored corners as they cleaned the rooms, and did not dust the tops of the picture frames.

"I declare I would be expending less energy if I did it myself," she said to Bess, "but I have to help Joss as well as teaching. Perhaps, now that fees have been paid for the boys, we can get a boy to help Joss. Perhaps that would be more fitting."

However all household worries vanished as she began to teach the boys and with the first response which she gained from them, her pleasure in the task grew so that joy and relief filled her heart. She could not teach housewifery, but she could teach knowledge. Nanny had to insist that they paused for their morning milk and mid-day meal, otherwise Judith might have forgotten the hour. Nanny had taken on the task of building up the health of the delicate boys and every empty plate was now a triumph for her. She insisted that meal times be kept.

Gradually the boys grew used to the

countryside and the widely differing landscape from that to which they were accustomed. And as they ventured into the garden, exploring the orchard and playing in the shrubbery, it began to shrink in size and soon they were looking at the rough ground and the fells which lay beyond, and Judith was secretly delighted to see their timid looks begin to vanish, and the eagerness of adventure take their place.

Nanny had tended to fill their heads with her tales of the wild dog of Ennerdale which had killed the sheep and terrorized the neighbourhood when she was a girl, she having lived for some years in Ennerdale. Also there were wild cats out on the fells which, if they were challenged, could bite a person to the bone. Three pairs of huge widened eyes listened to her stories avidly. Only when Judith overhead young Sam entreating her to tell them again about the boggle, did she interfere and forbid Nanny to fill their heads with such nonsense.

As the boys grew more energetic,

Judith began to take them into the rough field which adjoined Burroughs Park, and as they grew more and more used to the terrain, the boys began to enjoy running wild on this ground. It was full of adventure for them. Judith taught them to respect the wild life they found there and to be careful of the larger boulders in case they fell whilst climbing them and did themselves an injury.

All three boys loved 'the meadow' as they called it, and Judith began to use it as reward for good work accomplished.

"If you finish your arithmetic early," she would promise, "Miss Elizabeth and I will take you for an extra half-hour to the meadow."

Three pairs of eyes would light up and the work would progress at a spanking pace. It would be stupid to be deprived of extra time in the meadow because of a few sums. The boys learned, and Judith was delighted.

But Nanny began to find her task

a little more difficult. Now that their appetites had become unusually healthy and they were eating like young horses, their clothing was not only showing signs of wear, but it was fast becoming scarcely adequate to cover their growing bodies. In order to save their boots, they were allowed to go barefoot, and in order to save their fine jackets and coats, they were allowed to wear simple shirts.

"They look like village children," said Bess.

Judith pursed her mouth. "Their parents will no doubt inform us if they intend to visit Greyfells," she said. "Nanny will then prepare a bath for them and will clothe them properly. Besides, they are properly dressed for church each Sunday."

"That is so," said Bess, doubtfully, "but I hope no one of importance sees them when they play in the meadow."

It was part of Bess's duties to supervise the boys at play when Judith was busy with other things, but on one occasion she had left them to their games and returned to the house to finish a piece of sewing.

Later she had returned to the meadow to find all three boys full of good spirits and delicious fatigue after their taste of complete freedom. Unknown to Judith, who was busily preparing further lessons, and marking their written work, this became normal practice until Nanny Sherman came to find her, one day, and to tell her that Mr. Carrock had brought the boys home and they were all in the kitchen because Mr. Carrock would not allow them to venture into any other room in the house.

"I think they've been in the wee beck, Miss Judith," said Nanny, fearfully. "They are wet, all three, and Mr. Carrock . . . well . . . he doesn't seem in the best of tempers."

Alarm filled Judith's eyes as Nanny gave her this information.

"Where is Miss Bess?" she asked.

"She was in her room a wee while

back," Nanny said, rather slowly. "She has been a bit . . . well . . . indisposed today."

"We are *all* indisposed at *some* time," said Judith with some asperity. "Miss Bess should not leave the boys unsupervised. I had better see Mr. Carrock."

* * *

It was surely the worst afternoon of her whole life, thought Judith, if one did not include the nightmare time when her parents had been killed. If she had ever wondered what Mr. Carrock might look like when consumed with rage, she knew now. But she did her best to face him bravely.

"I understand, Miss Taverner, that *you* are in charge of these young hooligans," he said, icily.

"They are my pupils, sir."

"And what, may I ask, are you teaching them? How to be completely uncontrolled and unworthy as future citizens of their country?"

"I teach them basic subjects, sir, but for an hour each day they are allowed their freedom, though under supervision, in the meadow . . . *my* field which you have already coveted!"

He appeared to be breathing very deeply.

"Miss Taverner, I take it these young boys have parents who have no wish to dispose of their offspring . . . or have they found a very subtle assassin for unwanted children in you!"

She stared. "I fail to understand you, sir. If you are inferring that the children are not supervised, then you are quite wrong. They are delicate boys . . . "

"*Delicate* boys!" he hooted. "Miss Taverner, I cannot believe my ears! How can you claim these boys are delicate? I tell you, they are young hooligans. I found them near the crag on *my* land, and chased them until they fell in the beck."

"Then you should be ashamed, sir," she cried. "Why, all my good work, and Nanny's, will be lost if they catch a chill. We are building up their health, along with their education. That is what I am trying to do in my new school. I am only accepting delicate boys whose health will be improved at Greyfells, even as I teach them basic education. My sister supervises their play, but she had to return to the house to deal with a private matter. She would have returned to collect the boys within minutes of your finding them, I am quite sure. They were not likely to come to any harm."

"No harm!" cried Mr. Carrock, his voice roaring in his fury. "I must *insist* that they do not go near my land again."

"They were doing no harm."

"I have started to mine for lead, having found a rich seam on my land. There will be a great deal of heavy work being carried out during the next few weeks, and thereafter. May I leave it to your imagination, ma'am, to judge whether or not three energetic boys will be in no danger from such an enterprise? There will be blasting carried out at the mine, and heavy traffic with the removal of the ore, which is the reason why I offered for your field. It would have helped me to lay a straight track in order to join up with the main railway near Cockermouth. Do you think there is no danger for unsupervised boys?"

Judith's face had gone very white.

"You did not inform me of this, sir," she accused. "How could I know of this danger if you give me no reason for requiring my field? I, also, require the field. It is building up the health of my delicate boys."

"Damn the delicate boys!" he cried. "I tell you, there is nothing delicate about them. They are normal adventurous young rascals, and they will be the greatest nuisance to me in my project. I must ask you to give me your promise that they will never be allowed near the crags."

She wanted to shout at him equally

loudly, that he would never have such a promise from her, but her tongue was stilled. He had the upperhand. Now that she knew there was danger for the boys on Mr. Carrock's land, she could not allow them to venture near the mine.

Nanny had already removed the boys, and Bess, who had been extremely alarmed by the shouting between her sister and Mr. Carrock, helped her to clean them up and put on fresh clothing.

"I . . . it will all have to be considered," she prevaricated.

"I will have your promise, Miss Taverner," he said, quietly, "else I ascertain the names and addresses of the parents of your charges and inform them of the risk they run by leaving their sons in your care."

He could do so quite easily, thought Judith. She had no idea how he employed his spies, but they were very efficient. He had known, almost to a penny, the extent of her mortgage, and how the repayments were being made. Finding out the whereabouts of the Forsyths and the Dicksons would be child's play to Mr. Carrock.

Her face was very white as she looked at him.

"You leave me no alternative, sir, but to give you that promise," she said, in a low voice, "but I must have the use of the field near the house. It is ideal for children as a play area."

He was silent and once again his eyes began to sweep round the room.

"*Must* you take on this work, Miss Judith?" he asked, his voice now much quieter and more gentle. "It is a difficult task for a young lady . . . two young ladies."

Her face had warmed. "I enjoy teaching, Mr. Carrock. Please believe me that the boys have much improved since they came to me. Peter and Sam Forsyth are twins and have been delicate since birth, and Matthew Dickson had a winter cold which refused to go away. Now all three are much improved in health."

"I believe you. Very well, Miss Judith, tomorrow I will send two strong maidservants to clean up Greyfells for you. Your village maids are lazy sluts."

Her colour deepened. "They are working much better, but . . . but I cannot teach and . . . and supervise the maids."

He rubbed his forehead and looked exasperated.

"I will take care of that for you. Where are the children?"

They were all very subdued, in the small morning room, but Judith asked Nanny to bring them in. Mr. Carrock surveyed them keenly, noting the tight clothing and sun-fresh young faces. Matthew's cold had long since disappeared and even little Sam had a sprinkling of freckles on his small snub nose.

"You three youngsters cannot go further than the boulder which I showed you," Mr. Carrock said, firmly. "It is dangerous. Do you understand, young sirs? Dangerous. You could be blown to Eternity."

Sam paled. The other two moved restlessly.

"Do you enjoy being at school here, with Miss Taverner?"

All three nodded in unison. "Yes, sir," Peter croaked.

"Yes, sir," Matthew agreed. Sam dared not speak. He could not express how he felt about Greyfells.

"If you do not heed me, then you will obliged to return to your homes," said Mr. Carrock, clearly. "You understand?"

Again they nodded.

"You will all require to be supervised," he went on, looking at Bess who blushed and dropped her eyes.

"Goodday, then, Miss Judith . . . Miss Taverner. Goodday, Miss Elizabeth." He stared again at the children. "Delicate boys," he murmured, and made a sound which might have been stifled laughter.

8

M R. CARROCK'S visit had disconcerted Judith and for a few days she kept strict control over the boys. Bess, too, had been alarmed out of her lethargy, and was now more energetic in carrying out her own duties.

Judith and Nanny were very concerned because suddenly the boys had begun to grow like young trees, and their clothing no longer fitted. Nanny had tried to alter their garments by moving buttons and letting out seams until Judith became impatient.

"I shall write to the parents," she said, briskly. "After all, surely it is a mark of success that the boys are growing stouter. They should be happy to provide extra clothing for their sons."

"That would be a relief, Miss Judith," said Nanny. "I must say, young Master

Sam is filling out. He is not such a poor lad now."

Nanny had been less enthusiastic about the two maidservants who were sent over from Burroughs Park to serve Miss Taverner for a day or two. Judith felt rather offended and would have preferred not to have them in the house, but the maidservants appeared to have great respect for Mr. Carrock's wishes and Judith shrugged and washed her hands of it. They made a great deal of inconvenience in the house, but when they returned to Burroughs Park, they left a sweet-smelling house behind them, and Judith was resolved to maintain the same high standard.

* * *

Mrs. Simon Carrock, who insisted that Judith must remember to call her Françoise, drove over one fine afternoon. The sun was shining and the rippling waters of Lake Bassenthwaite sparkled like diamonds, with the towering peaks of Skiddaw, pale misty blue against the clearer blue of the sky, making a breath-taking picture of great natural beauty.

"It ees ver' pretty," said Françoise. "I remember it when I go home."

"Are you going home soon?" Judith asked.

"Not yet. Only when my dearest Simon say so. Maman is better and my dearest Simon comes to stay nex' week, and Aidan promises entertainment. We have a beeg party at Burroughs Park, and we dance. You will have invitation, and Mees Bess. Aidan sends you invitation. Maman is writing them. She likes the entertainment."

Judith looked at her with consternation.

"Oh, but . . . but we do not dance," she objected.

"Oh, Judith! You know we do not dance because there are few opportunities," Bess objected.

"We are too busy, Bess," said Judith, firmly.

"You will get invitations," said Françoise, standing up to leave. "You will come to the party. It is expected of you, and all will be arranged. Aidan will send carriage for two."

As she sauntered to the door, Françoise looked back, a half smile lighting up her dark eyes.

"The other neighbour, Monsieur Mardale, also gets the invitation," she said, turning to look at them like a sleepy cat.

Judith stared. "Mr. Mardale?" she repeated, "of Hazlemont?"

Hazlemont was a larger estate than Greyfells, but not nearly so large as Burroughs Park. Mr. and Mrs. Mardale were now elderly people who took little part in the social life of the community, their estate being run by a manager who lived with his wife and family in the cothouse.

"But . . . but Mr. Mardale is now over seventy years old."

"I do not mean the old one. I mean the young M. Mardale. I theenk he calls himself Jonathan. He is grandson to the old ones. His father and mother live in India, but he comes home to be with the old ones."

"I had not heard," said Judith while Bess, too, shook her head.

"It makes no matter," said Françoise. "I tell you because all the neighbours will come. You, too."

Judith watched her go, her eyes sober as she turned to Bess who obviously found the thought of such a party very exciting.

"Of course we can go, Judy," she cried. "We are out of mourning. Françoise is quite right. It *is* expected of us. If Mr. Mardale can go, we can."

"What shall we wear?" asked Judith. "Have you thought about *that*, Bess?"

The pleasure began to fade from Bess's face, and again the ready tears started to well in her eyes.

"It is not fair!" she cried. "You spoil everything for me, Judith. Just when I think I am going to enjoy something, you . . . you keep reminding me how poor we are. Why shouldn't we have some money for new gowns?"

"Who will pay the mortgage if we use the money for gowns?"

"Bother the old mortgage. Who receives our money, anyway? Could we not appeal to him to forego, just for *one* month?"

"It isn't *one* person," said Judith, patiently, "it's a bank, or a finance house . . . some sort of corporation to which the money is paid by young Mr. Brent. No, we cannot appeal to forego, even for one month. Oh Bess, I *am* sorry, my dear, I know it is hard and you are young . . ."

"Do not keep trying to help, Judith," Bess cried. "It isn't fair! I want to go to the party, and I *am* going, somehow!"

She rushed upstairs and Judith sighed and prepared to call the boys for their next lesson. Soon they would be going home, but on the success of this project rested a future life for Bess and herself. If the parents of her boys were satisfied, she would ask for recommendations and on these she would launch her school on a very professional basis.

But what would happen, she wondered, if she could not find more delicate boys who required to be educated? Far from worrying about parties, she and Bess might be worrying about keeping a roof over their heads!

★ ★ ★

The invitation arrived a few days later and it was Nanny Sherman who brought a bit of hope to Bess, and even to Judith.

"I don't like to put this idea forward, Miss Judith, except that you are both my bairns and I would like to see you having a bit of fun for a little while. But have you thought about your dear mama's gowns? Mrs. Taverner was always very well dressed and her gowns are still in the wardrobes. I am sure they could be altered in a style to suit you and Miss Bess."

Judith's eyes widened with the thought.

114

She had left her mother's clothes untouched, thinking that a day would come when she would be able to look at them dispassionately. Even now she knew that it would not be easy to examine her mother's wardrobe. Her sweet delicate perfume might still cling to the clothes, and Judith's heart ached at the thought. She had forced herself to be hard in order to face her problems, but even now it would be so easy to collapse into a storm of weeping.

But Bess was looking at her so hopefully.

"Very well," she said, huskily, "we will look at . . . at mother's gowns. There is a fine sempstress in Keswick and we could take them there for alteration. I expect we could afford that where we could not afford new gowns. The only thing is . . . Nanny, would you be able to attend to the boys?"

"Bless you, Miss Judith, I am still good enough to keep those three young rascals in good behaviour. You need not worry your head about them!"

Suddenly Judith felt a lightening of her spirits such as she had not experienced this many a day.

"Very good, Nanny. Tomorrow morning we go through our mother's wardrobe, and if we find anything suitable, why then we might attend the party at Burroughs Park."

Bess rushed to throw her arms round her sister's neck.

"Oh, Judy! Isn't it exciting?"

"It is only fitting," said Nanny Sherman, "that you two young ladies should be enjoying your young lives and taking your rightful place in the community. You are both entitled to go to the ball, more than anyone. It is only fitting, Miss Judith."

Bess turned to Judith as they went upstairs to bed that evening.

"I wonder what Mr. Jonathan Mardale is like," she said. "I did not know that old Mr. and Mrs. Mardale had a grandson."

"I have not heard him mentioned,"

said Judith, shrugging. She did not think it was important and had no idea how wrong that would prove to be.

There were several ball gowns which were suitable, with necessary alterations, for both Bess and Judith, and it was Bess who claimed first choice. She had always been more interested in clothing than her older sister.

"I like this creamy silk," she said, holding a rich, elegantly-styled gown with a low-cut neckline, the skirt embroidered with seed pearls and brilliants, against her slender body. "However, perhaps I ought to choose pink, or . . . or does the blue suit me best, Judy?"

"What?"

Judith's thoughts had been elsewhere. That morning she had received a letter from old Mr. Brent saying that part of their income would have to be cut because one of their investments was paying poor dividends. Judith's heart sank. It was a blow, just when every penny counted. She was having to force herself to take an interest in the forthcoming social occasion.

"Oh . . . the gowns . . . yes, I think the blue for you, Bess," she decided.

If Mr. Carrock was *not* married after all, would he be such a bad match for Bess? Truly they had started badly with Mr. Carrock, and she had been furiously angry with him because she had felt he had insulted her and Bess, with the help of Françoise. But he must have grown tired of receiving so many young ladies with marriage in mind, and he had been quite correct in introducing Françoise as Mrs. Carrock. She was, after all, Mrs. Simon Carrock. No, she could not blame him too much, with so many match-makers . . .

Judith caught her breath and her cheeks warmed. She was just as busy as anyone in trying to catch him for her sister. But if only Bess could marry well . . .

"The blue," she said, decisively, "yes . . . it does make your eyes look lovely, Bess."

"Which for you?" Bess asked, pleased. The blue had a lovely sweeping skirt, trimmed with forget-me-nots.

"Oh, any . . . that cream silk will do very well. I do not need a colour because I do not wish to attract attention. I shall be happy to chaperone you."

Judith was kept very busy during the next few days with her teaching and her household management. She must not allow Greyfells to become lax once more. She also wanted the boys to do neat written work to show their parents in order to collect good recommendations from them. Perhaps she could take six boys now, instead of three, and her income would be doubled. That would more than compensate for poor investments.

The thought cheered her so that when she and Bess prepared for the ball at Burroughs Park, Judith became affected by her sister's excitement, and her eyes shone so that her face became unusually beautiful as she pinned up her shining dark brown curls, and Nanny Sherman helped to do up the hooks of her gown.

"Oh, Miss Judith!" she said. "It does suit you! Why, you look . . . "

Nanny could not find words. Often she had sighed over Miss Judith, thinking her rather a plain young lady and that she might find it difficult to catch a husband, but now she was astonished to see that the young lady looked very handsome. It was not the usual pretty looks which were so much admired, but something about Miss Judith drew one's eyes to her. The gown had been pulled in at the waist to suit her slender figure, and pretty lace set into the neckline so that it was not so low-cut for an unmarried lady. The sempstress had also added matching lace to the sleeves and it had softened up Miss Judith's looks so that she seemed delicate and slender. Nanny buttoned her young lady's hands into long white kid gloves and she had found a creamy silk shawl for Miss

Judith and a soft white woollen shawl for Miss Bess.

Bess looked enchanting in her blue gown, but she, too had been struck by Judith's glowing looks and felt quite put out when she saw how well the cream silk looked on her sister.

"I suppose you remembered which was Mama's *best* gown," she remarked, a trifle sulkily. "I think it *was* that silk, Judith. Yet you encouraged me to choose the blue."

But for once Judith was impatient with her sister.

"You had first choice, Bess," she said, briskly. "You could have chosen this one quite easily. In any case, the blue is perfect for you and you know you are much prettier than I. Françoise is sending the carriage for the two of us. Our own is not quite the thing for such an occasion."

The boys were allowed to see them dressed in their ball gowns and for once all three were silent with admiration, then Sam spoke up.

"Are you fairy princesses tonight?" he asked. "Will you be Miss Judith and Miss Bess tomorrow once more?"

Judith laughed. "That is so, Sam," she agreed. "Come, Bess, here is the carriage arriving for us now."

9

BURROUGHS PARK looked wonderfully festive with garlands of flowers and greenery decorating the great hall and reception rooms, whilst soft music was being played from a dais in the corner of the music room.

Mr. Aidan Carrock looked very distinguished in black velvet with snow-white lace on his shirt and diamond-studded buttons on his coat. Beside him stood Françoise and Madame de Ridieux, with Mr. Simon Carrock, waiting to greet their guests.

Françoise looked very beautiful in a white gown embroidered with silver thread whilst Madame de Ridieux was very stately in dark purple lace, a magnificent necklace of amethysts and diamonds encircling her neck. She had only a very few words of

English, but when she found that Judith could converse with her in her own tongue, she revealed a lightness of spirit at variance with her more sombre appearance.

At first glance, also, Mr. Simon Carrock seemed an unlikely choice of husband for Françoise. He was not so tall as his brother, and perhaps a little more heavily built, but his face was strong and full of intelligence, and as he and Judith were introduced, his eyes grew suddenly keen and she was aware of his scrutiny, then he smiled and she could see that he was a very attractive man.

Judith was also aware that she was attracting the attention of other guests and her cheeks grew warm with embarrassment. She began to believe that the cream silk gown had been a dreadful error. She was used to less noticeable attire, and to merging into the background. She was unaware that her own looks were outstanding and many who had dismissed the elder

Miss Taverner as being unfortunate in looks, were now astonished by her undoubted beauty.

Mr. Carrock's gaze, too, had swept over her from head to foot, but she could not be sure of his approval. For once there was nowhere to hide. The dress ensured that she could be easily distinguished amongst other young ladies.

Then Judith forgot to be self-conscious, and indeed forgot about her own appearance as, later in the evening, Françoise came to introduce Mr. Jonathan Mardale of Hazlemont, and Judith found herself gazing at surely the most handsome young man she had ever seen. His looks were comparable to the heroes of Greek literature which she enjoyed so much, and every eye in the room had been turned in his direction. He had been finishing his education at Oxford University, and it had been decided that he should journey north to spend a few months with his grandparents at Hazlemont before joining his parents in India.

"My father serves the Raj," he explained to Judith, "and I may travel back to India as Ensign Mardale, but that has still to be decided. Meanwhile my father desires me to support my grandparents in his absence. My grandfather has grown feeble in recent years. I was greatly bored by the idea, but I must say, Miss Taverner, that I had no idea we had such charming neighbours."

His smile included Bess, who blushed prettily.

"We must stand up together when there is dancing, and if I may be allowed to dance with Miss Elizabeth, also, why then it will be an evening to remember."

It was an evening of enchantment for Judith. She forgot about everyone else, and even forgot to worry about Bess, as she danced with young Mr. Mardale and enjoyed the attentions of other young men before dancing with him again.

Only Mr. Carrock appeared to be in a sober mood at his own party. He, too, danced with Judith and somehow his very proximity brought her back to earth with a bump. Tomorrow this wonderful, magical, fairy-tale world of flowers, music, candle-light, beauty and enchantment would all be gone. It would vanish with the removal of the cream silk gown which had become, for a little while, the most natural apparel in the world. Tomorrow she would go back to teaching the boys and to worrying about how to find more pupils when they returned to their homes once more.

"The dreams are leaving your eyes," said Aidan Carrock, rather brusquely. "Have I chased them away, Miss Judith?"

"It is almost midnight," she said. "Surely that is when they will vanish."

"Perhaps they need not," said Mr. Carrock, a note of meaning in his voice, and the last drop of joy in the evening faded. He was, of course, referring to her stubborn refusal to sell him her field. If she accepted his generous offer, then things would undoubtedly be easier for her and she might have time to dream for a little longer before the nightmare started once more.

But just for one night, it would have been nice to forget about everyday worries. She looked around, seeing that Bess was dancing with Mr. Mardale, then she turned to look at Aidan Carrock.

"Perhaps it is a timely reminder, sir, that my sister and I should go home before our coach changes to a pumpkin."

His eyes hardened as he followed her gaze.

"Surely you can afford a little more time on such an evening," he said. "Would you spoil your sister's pleasure in order to satisfy your own sense of propriety?"

"Hardly that, sir! You forget that we have to work for our bread."

"I have forgotten nothing," he said,

quietly. "I only hope there has not been too much stardust sprinkled around you this evening."

His eyes had again flickered towards Bess and Mr. Mardale. Was he warning her that Mr. Mardale was hardly likely to wish to pursue a friendship with two penniless young ladies, even if they *were* neighbours? He was being very practical, of course, but Judith began to feel that all her misfortunes seemed to be personified by this man. Everything around her was like a bubble of brightness and hope, a world full of happiness and laughter. But Mr. Carrock rose up, tall and dark, to remind her of the realities of her life.

"I shall find my sister, Mr. Carrock," she said, quietly. "We will return home now."

"I shall let you know when the carriage has been arranged for both of you," he said, gently. "Miss Taverner, I would like the pleasure of calling upon you shortly, to discuss a matter of some importance."

"I shall not sell," she said, in a low voice. "Do not remind me of such a dull matter, Mr. Carrock. I shall not sell, not even to help with my mortgage."

"We shall see. Perhaps we can discuss that mortgage."

"It has nothing to do with you!" she said, angrily.

"It has everything to do with me, since I hold it, Miss Judith."

Her face went very white and he gripped her hand tightly.

"Did you *really* not know about that? Has it not been explained to you by your solicitors? Please do not upset yourself, Miss Judith . . . "

"Ah, you are here, *chérie* . . . "

"Françoise came up and accosted them, her voice delicious with laughter.

"Come," she said, "it is now the dance where we change partners, and my dearest Simon weeshes to standup with Judith, my frien'. Dearest Aidan will dance with me."

"I . . . I am fatigued," said Judith,

130

rather faintly, but she had no time for more as she was obliged to dance with Mr. Simon Carrock.

"If you are, indeed, fatigued then we will sit down and I shall find you some refreshment, Miss Taverner," he said, formally. "I owe you my thanks and I would be happy to express it in any small service I can do for you."

"For what, sir?"

"You have kept my dear wife entertained, *and* her mother. It is lonely for her when she speaks no English! Soon my duties will be over and Françoise and Madame de Ridieux will come to London for a month or two, then perhaps Paris, before we return to Martinique. But she might have been lonely and dull here at Burroughs Park, had it not been for you."

"I have done nothing," said Judith, uncomfortably, seeing the amusement in his eyes. "It is she who has cheered me, Mr. Carrock."

"And you have enjoyed this evening

which she has arranged with such determination? She specially wished you to be happy."

Judith's eyes flickered towards Mr. Aidan Carrock's tall figure, seeing that his eyes sought hers constantly. Then she caught sight of Mr. Mardale and she knew that the evening had had great significance for her, even though Mr. Carrock had shattered her enjoyment, and perhaps the last vestige of peace of mind. She would never forget dancing and talking with Mr. Mardale, even if she never saw him again.

"It has been a memorable evening, Mr. Simon," she said, honestly.

She felt her life would never be quite the same again.

★ ★ ★

It was difficult to prize Bess away from the ball before the last guest had left Burroughs Park, but Judith was in no mood to indulge her sister too much.

"But there may be yet one more

dance, Judy," Bess implored. "Perhaps Mr. Mardale will look for me."

"*No* more dances, Bess. We will say goodnight to our host and hostesses, Mr. Carrock and his relatives, and be on our way. The carriage is being arranged."

"You are just jealous," said Bess, peevishly, "because Mr. Mardale has danced more dances with me, than with you."

Judith wanted to slap her.

"I told you, Mr. Carrock has ordered the carriage for the two of us. We will be in breach of good manners if we do not go . . . now!"

Bess knew when to stop arguing, and they said their goodnights, and walked out into a night so bright with moonlight that the trees threw long fantastic shadows on to the park which was lit with strange blue ghostly light. The stars were so clearly defined and so low that they might have been diamonds escaping from the jewellery worn by the ladies.

"Mr. Mardale will call on me tomorrow," said Bess, blissfully, as they descended from the carriage and walked into Greyfells.

"He will no doubt wish to call on *both* of us," said Judith, and Bess's eyes narrowed.

"I was correct. You *are* jealous," she said, her mouth tightening.

"I am tired," said Judith, "and I have no time for your childish tantrums tonight, Bess. I hope you told Mr. Mardale that we are not always free during the day."

"You spoil everything!" cried Bess. "I wanted to forget about that."

"So did I," Judith returned.

In spite of her weariness, sleep eluded her and constantly she saw, in her mind's eye, the Grecian profile of Mr. Jonathan Mardale, then his warm smile as he turned towards her, making her aware of herself as a woman for the first time in her life.

Then the dark stern gaze of Aidan Carrock would intrude, and with it would come the nightmare knowledge that he held the mortgage on Greyfells. Was it true? How could it be true? Yet she knew it must be so, or he would not have said it. Her father must have borrowed from Hugo Carrock, and the repayments would no doubt be made by her solicitors to Mr. Carrock's bank. She should have been informed about this, but old Mr. Brent was trying to make things easy for her and fully believed that she did not understand financial matters. She would make an appointment with young Mr. Brent and ask him to explain every detail of her situation, down to the last farthing.

But first of all, Mr. Carrock was going to call on her to discuss some sort of business arrangement. What could it be? He wanted more of her land, but he was not going to get it . . . not going to get it . . .

She slept, but woke late next morning, feeling very unrefreshed.

10

MR. JONATHON MARDALE rode over to Greyfells the following morning and threw Nanny Sherman into a turmoil when he begged leave to see Miss Taverner, and Miss Elizabeth. In the cold light of day, his good looks were even more striking, but Judith thought that her own had suffered considerably now that she was once again wearing her grey gown with the plain white collar and cuffs.

Bess still looked enchanting in pink and white checked gingham, and her cheeks were flushed with excitement. She had anticipated the visit and had taken more care than usual with pinning up her fair hair.

At first Judith demurred about the propriety of the visit, especially when she, herself, was so busy in the schoolroom, but her heart was beating much faster than usual, and she could not keep the excitement from her eyes.

"I have asked the gentleman to wait in the drawing room, Miss Judith," said Nanny.

"And he asked to speak to me . . . and Miss Elizabeth?"

"Very true, Miss Judith. The young gentleman asked if he could be honoured by speaking to both of you."

Judith smoothed down her dress.

"Very well, Nanny. Could you ask Miss Bess to join us in the drawing room and . . . er . . . perhaps a little Madeira and a ratafia biscuit?"

The Madeira was used most sparingly and Nanny's eyes were speculative as she looked at Miss Judith. She was showing her agitation in the way her fingers plucked at her gown, and Miss Judith was always such a calm young lady. Truly, however, the young gentleman was very handsome and it was plain that Miss Bess thought so, too. Nanny shook her head as she went to deliver her message. She hoped there would not be jealousy between her two young ladies. That would not make things very easy.

Judith was enchanted with Jonathan Mardale, especially when he understood so quickly about her delicate boys, and her reason for turning Greyfells into such a school.

"I think it is a wonderful enterprise, Miss Taverner," he enthused, then turned to Bess.

"And you are also part of the project, Miss Elizabeth?"

Bess's eyes were shining as though lit with an inner glow, and for a brief moment Judith felt a touch of irritation. Surely Bess should not show such open admiration for Mr. Mardale! He was interested in *her* project, and she had felt his interest in *her* from their first meeting. But Bess was very susceptible to male attention when it was from someone so . . . so presentable. It rarely lasted for long.

"I . . . I teach music and . . . and art," she was saying with many blushes.

"How *very* accomplished," said Mr. Mardale, "and how kind of you both to spare a few minutes of your time. It has been rather lonely for me at Hazlemont since my grandparents rarely leave the house and do not entertain. But I do not wish to keep you from your task, Miss Taverner," he said, turning to Judith. "I wonder . . . would it be presumptuous of me to ask if I could help in any way? I would be glad to talk to your young pupils about life in India, both from the point of view of a poor boy, and one who has been born into a wealthy family."

"Oh, Mr. Mardale, what a wonderful idea!" cried Judith, happily. "May I announce such a treat to the pupils, and let them know when you might be free to come?"

"Shall we say Friday afternoon, Miss Taverner?"

Again he turned to Bess.

"Would that be a convenient time

for you, too, Miss Elizabeth?"

"I would look forward to it greatly," said Bess, shyly.

"It would be of great benefit, I'm sure," said Judith.

How handsome he was, she thought, her eyes on his strong, yet boyish face. His hair curled close to his head, and his profile was most handsome in a truly classical fashion. For a brief moment it crossed her mind that she ought to be circumspect with him. She and Bess were surely greatly honoured to have such a fine young man offering a ready hand of friendship, but her pleasure in him was too great to be spoiled by such thoughts. He was, after all, a neighbour just as Mr. Carrock was a neighbour. It was perfectly correct for them to take pleasure in his company.

Judith was very conscious of her rather toil-worn hands, compared with Bess's tiny pink and white delicate fingers as Mr. Mardale took leave of them. She would like to have sat down quietly in a chair and perhaps dreamed a little, but there was no time. Nanny Sherman was keeping an eye on the boys, and it was time for their next lesson. Matthew and Peter plodded their way through their lessons, but Sam's bright eyes would light up with intelligence and Judith found him a joy to teach.

Bess was humming a little as she made her way towards the stairs prior to going up to her room and the sound inexplicably irritated Judith.

"Bess, it would be more correct if you were not so forward with your answers to Mr. Mardale," she said, crisply. "He does us great honour by offering his help like this. We must accept it with due decorum."

Bess's eyes sparkled with indignation.

"I was not forward!" she said, angrily. "I think *you* were forward with Mr. Mardale, Judith. In fact, I was in some embarrassment to see your eagerness to please."

This time Judith's cheeks flushed. *Had* she been too open in her pleasure at Mr. Mardale's visit? Surely she had not!

"I hope I know my manners," she said, with dignity. "After all, *he* called to see *me*. I did not influence him into this visit."

"He came to see *me*," cried Bess, adding a little belatedly, " . . . also."

"I think it would be a mistake to expect too much of his interest," said Judith.

"I agree with you, sister," said Bess, "but he *did* express to me the hope that he would like to call on me at Greyfells, and would do so with all propriety. That meant he should also call upon *you*, since you are my older sister, and guardian."

"Of course he would do so," said Judith, swiftly. "He is a gentleman of some sense. That is why we must treat him as such. I will go and tell the boys that they have a treat in store. In the meantime, I shall try to find a map of India, and teach the boys a little of its geography. That should make Mr. Mardale's talk even more interesting."

Bess said no more, but she rushed on upstairs. On other occasions Judith had known her to burst into tears when she was corrected, but this time Bess's whole attitude was one of anger and defiance. Judith sighed. She hoped that Bess was not going to become more difficult than usual. If . . . if *someone* offered for her, Judith, in marriage (and such a thing had never before been contemplated since she had not thought she could attract a man), but if *someone* offered for her, then she did not want to be handicapped by having a difficult sister in her charge. Bess's manners would have to be corrected daily so that she would learn how to think of others besides herself.

★ ★ ★

Mr. Mardale's visit had so entranced Judith that she had put to the back of her mind the shock of discovering that Mr. Carrock held the mortgage on Greyfells. She had even forgotten that Mr. Carrock had intimated that he wished to call on her very soon on a matter of business, but she was very soon reminded of this visit on the following afternoon when Nanny Sherman once again came to find her.

"It would seem that we are popular with the gentlemen, Miss Judith," she said, drily. "Mr. Aidan Carrock enquires for you. I have put him in the drawing room. I do not think the small business room very comfortable for such an important personage, Miss Judith."

Judith sighed and laid aside her pencil where she had been correcting the work of her pupils. Bess was now teaching them art, and had been surprisingly amenable over taking the lesson. In fact, Bess appeared to be gaining in dignity, and her appearance was also greatly enhanced by new care and attention. Her hair was well brushed and curled, and her gowns fresh every day, and protected by a large apron which could be removed at a moment's notice.

Judith had marked these improvements and voiced her approval. Having few gowns of her own, she had once again searched her mother's wardrobe for more sober gowns and had altered two of them to suit her own slender figure.

One of these, in a deep rich shade of sapphire blue, enhanced her eyes and made her complexion look as smooth as rich cream. She wore it now as she went to pay her respect to Mr. Carrock and saw that his eyes flickered over her appreciatively as she walked into the room and he rose to his feet, towering over her.

But again she was conscious of her roughed hands as he held out his own, and she saw him frown as he turned her hand over and held it for a second longer than was necessary before releasing it.

"It is good of you to see me,

Miss Judith," he said, rather roughly, and with surprise she realised he was a trifle nervous.

"Not at all, sir," she said, quietly. "It would seem that . . . you have a certain right to my time whenever it is necessary. I will contact my solicitors but I know that you hold the mortgage on Greyfells. I would like to remind you, however, that while I meet the repayments, you cannot force me to do anything I do not wish to do, such as selling you my field. I shall only allow the smallest part of Greyfells to be sold now if we are in dire need."

"Admirable sentiments," said Mr. Carrock, quietly, "though I do feel that the particular field we have in mind would not deplete your land by many acres. Mining for lead is now under way on my property and we may have to use gunpowder. I would prefer to own all lands near the workings of my mine, and . . ."

"No, Mr. Carrock, please do not pursue the matter. If I sold that

146

field to you, it would cut through the boundaries of my land."

"Please allow me to finish, Miss Judith," he said and again she saw that he was nervous. "I have something else I wish to discuss with you which may, or may not of course, have a bearing on the matter."

He paused and she waited expectantly as he began to prowl up and down the room. He was very tall and dark, she thought, looking up at him, but not nearly so handsome as Mr. Mardale. His features were too strong. He reminded Judith of one of the huge golden eagles which nested in the mountains, as his eyes pierced her and he paced the floor warily.

"You have no relations, Miss Judith?" he asked. "I mean, if I wish to consult you on a . . . a private matter, I must talk with you alone, or is there someone I could approach who would have your interests at heart?"

"What do you mean?" she asked, alarmed. "I have no relatives. I *have* to manage my own affairs."

He stopped pacing and stared at her, then he smiled and she was struck by the change in his face. If only he would smile a little more often, perhaps they could even begin to like one another a little.

"I rather thought that was the way of it," he said very gently. "Very well, Miss Judith, then I will present my case to you. As you know, I have recently returned to Burroughs Park from the West Indies where my family had various business interests and other connections. I have a small estate on the island of Dominica where my brother was in Government service, also in Martinique. They were in our mother's family and are now administered by my brother and myself. My brother married a lady from Martinique . . . as you know . . . and he will return there in a few months. He will take over all our interests there. He wishes to leave the diplomatic service."

"That is . . . is interesting," said Judith, lamely, wondering what this intelligence could mean to her.

"I intend to remain in England permanently to look after Burroughs Park, and occasionally to go to London where I also have a home, and business interests, which can only be administered from London. I also intend to export some of the lead and zinc which are being mined on my land."

Judith inclined her head. Mr. Carrock's recital was rather halting and she was becoming somewhat disinterested in the catalogue of his affairs.

"I shall be living at Burroughs Park," he repeated, "and . . . " This time his cheeks flushed, " . . . and I find that I need a lady who would be the mistress of Burroughs Park and would run my household as it should be run. In short, I need a wife, Miss Judith, and I would like you to consider marriage to me. I am quite sure you will see immediately the advantages of such a position. I mean, you must have considered those when you brought Miss Bess to see me . . . "

Judith's face had flushed scarlet.

"No, do not be angry, I beg of you," he said, swiftly holding up his hand. "I admire you for doing your best for your sister and trying to find her a husband with property worthy of her. But, to continue, I know you must have assessed the advantages from your point of view, and from mine they are manifold. I do not wish . . . "

"You *do* wish to use me as . . . as some sort of preventative measure against match-making females besieging you with their female offspring of marriageable age," said Judith, furiously. "Mr. Carrock, I think you must believe me to be out of my mind. You must believe that I am a lunatic! Do you think I would marry for such a reason?"

"I would have thought that a *practical* approach would be more to your liking than a profession of love," said Mr. Carrock.

"Certainly it would be the only approach open to *you*, Mr. Carrock," said Judith. "You could not possibly believe I would be naïve enough to think you could ever love me. Or I you," she added.

"Marriage with me would have a great many advantages for you, Miss Judith," said Aidan Carrock, deciding to ignore any references to love. "I thought you would see those immediately. Perhaps I am explaining it all badly, and in any case, I know you would wish to have time to think over my proposal. I hope you will not consider the matter for *too* long, however, because I would like us to be married before my brother and sister-in-law return to Martinique. It would be a quiet affair, the ceremony being performed by the Reverend Stephen Laird, but Madame de Ridieux is very experienced in arranging these matters, and she would ensure that our wedding would be properly conducted. Do please think it over, Miss Judith."

Her face was very white, her blue eyes wide and shining like sapphires with agitation. How could he think she would ever want to marry him?

Yet would it have been so distasteful to her before Mr. Mardale arrived? a small voice whispered. She had wanted him for Bess, then she had been angered and embarrassed when he saw through her intentions, and she believed he was lying to her about Françoise. It had seemed such an excellent solution to her problems to have the master of Burroughs Park taking over her affairs.

In fact, even now it *would* be practical. She would not have to worry about the mortgage, or the servants, or even finding more pupils. There would be no problem over the field . . .

"Surely it is going to great lengths to acquire my field," she said, then wished the words unsaid when she saw that they had angered him.

"I would not have thought that remark worthy of you, Miss Taverner," he said, stiffly. "If you have gained that impression of me, then I can see that I am wasting my time." His eyes sparkled angrily. "I see you have decided to dress like a young lady and not an elderly crow. I cannot now believe that the change is intended to please my eyes. I hope it is not for Mardale's benefit. Take care that he is not casting his eyes in another direction."

Her chest heaved with rage.

"How dare you, Mr. Carrock! What a good thing that I did not immediately accept your proposal! I feel there is a great deal of you that I do not know, or understand, some of it surely spiteful."

He was biting his lip.

"I apologise," he muttered. "I had no right to say that to you. That is why I wish . . . I wish I could have talked this over with a relative of yours before approaching you. But . . . but please believe me when I say that I . . . I do have regard for you. I do not find this easy to say, or even to explain, but . . . but I do have regard for you."

Again his tone was very gentle and again she wanted to sit down and weep, though she hardly knew why. There was a great deal of Bess in her, she thought. Yet she despised the softness of tears, except on occasions of dire distress.

"I shall come back for your answer this day week," he said, as he began to take his leave. "I return to London tomorrow for several days. That will give you time to consider."

"I shall not change my mind, sir," she said, steadily.

"No? Well, perhaps not, but I would like you to consider the matter nevertheless."

"Else you will foreclose on the mortgage," she said, with a watery smile.

He blinked, then the smile once again lit up his face, and the weight of years seemed to fall away from him.

"That I shall," he promised. "I most certainly will foreclose on the mortgage."

He took both her hands in his and when she would have pulled them away, he gripped them more tightly when he examined them with keen eyes, and suddenly bent to kiss her fingers. A strange shiver shook her body at the touch of his lips.

"I am proud of these small hands," he said, softly, "but I would see that they grew beautiful once more, or that they remained workworn by your choice and not by necessity. I would take care of you, my dear."

Moments later he had gone and this time Judith sat alone in the drawing room and felt so confused that even the room she had known all her life seemed strange and was full of shadows. Mr. Carrock had offered for her! She had turned him down! Most of the women in the neighbourhood would never believe she had done such a thing. They would not even believe that she had *had* such an offer were she to shout it from the rooftops.

But she did not love Mr. Carrock. He was a strange man, full of darkness and secrets. He was not like Mr. Mardale who was full of light and on whom she could lavish so much love. She could not marry Mr. Carrock because she loved Mr. Mardale. She might as well be honest with herself.

Bess came softly into the room.

"What did Mr. Carrock want, Judith?" she asked, fearfully. "I heard your voices raised as though in anger. Has he threatened us?"

Judith shook her head.

"He . . . he offered for me," she said, wonderingly. "He wanted marriage."

"Marriage!" cried Bess, astonished. "With you! You mean that Mr. Carrock offered for . . . for you?"

"I have just said so," Judith replied, rather wearily.

"But . . . but . . . "

Bess took a second look at her

sister. That Mr. Aidan Carrock should offer for Judith! Were her unusual looks really attractive to a man? If so . . . what of Mr. Mardale? Could it be that Mr. Mardale really *did* find her sister's looks pleasing?

Bess felt greatly taken aback. She remembered how well Judith had looked at the ball. She had always believed that Judith would never be given the opportunity of marriage and now . . . now here she was being offered for by the most eligible man in the county. And if she married Mr. Carrock, why then . . . why then there was no need for concern . . .

Bess's face began to glow.

"Oh, Judith!" she cried. "I am so *very* happy for you. Do you not see? This will solve all of our problems. He would not be a good husband for me because he would grow bored with me. I would not talk to him and our minds would not be in tune. But . . . you! How different it would be with you! There would be companionship between you and out of that, love will grow."

Judith was staring at her sister.

"Do not run on, Bess," she said, quietly. "I do not intend to marry Mr. Carrock. He is no husband for me. I do not love him."

Bess's eyes flickered and she turned away. There was no need to argue further with Judith, and suddenly the situation was clear between them without laying it on the table for all to see. Judith could not love Mr. Carrock because already her heart was reaching out to Mr. Mardale.

Bess's childish face was no longer so young as she turned away. Her own heart was also touched by Mr. Mardale. Well, perhaps he would not look twice at either of them, but so long as he wished to call upon them and make himself pleasant to them, she would not retire into the background and leave everything clear for Judith. Perhaps she *was* the elder sister, but a whole lifetime stretched ahead of Bess and if she could share it with Mr. Mardale she would

158

not want more from this life.

"I think Nanny is preparing tea," she said, quietly. "I will offer my help, Judith."

In silence Judith watched her go.

11

MR. MARDALE'S lecture on India was greeted with pleasure by everyone at Greyfells. Judith invited Nanny to join her class of the three boys, together with Bess and herself. Mr. Mardale looked very smart and quietly competent when he arrived, his fresh white shirt contrasting with the well-cut coat of finest wool-cloth.

It was Judith who was nervous and excited as she introduced him to the boys, and with an ease of manner which she greatly admired, he walked up to the blackboard on which she had pinned a map of India, and began his talk by pointing out most of the large towns which he had visited from time to time, with special reference to his birthplace of Simla.

He then began to describe what it would be like to live in India if one were a poor boy, living one's life in the bazaars, and by contrast, the life of the eldest son of a maharajah.

"Perhaps you would like to be very rich," he said, "and to be able to ride on an elephant, wear rich clothing, go hawking or shooting wild animals, but your movements would be restricted by many servants employed to guard your safety on pain of great punishment if you were harmed in any way. You might grow lazy and fat and rather selfish if your every whim was indulged in this way.

"On the other hand, you could wake in the mornings feeling very hungry if you were a poor boy, and you might even try to commit the sin of stealing food in the bazaars and would be punished very severely if you were caught . . . as you would be at some time. Some boys, younger than yourselves, find work to do in the bazaars and live independent lives, looking after themselves and even helping their families. Perhaps you might prefer to be an English boy, being taught your letters by such fine teachers as Miss Taverner and Miss Elizabeth."

He went on to describe the climate and the wildlife, dwelling mostly on the beauty rather than the ugliness and his audience was uplifted by the enchantment of hearing about that country which seemed so very far away.

All too soon, however, the talk was ended and Judith set the children to write down all they could remember about India, whilst Bess decided that they could paint a picture of the beautiful mountainous scenery which Mr. Mardale had described.

Nanny Sherman prepared tea for the ladies and their guest, serving it in the drawing room whilst she and the boys ate home-made bread and strawberry jam with fresh creamy milk, in the schoolroom. Their appetites were now of the best, and their cheeks had grown rounded and glowed with health.

Mr. Mardale was unstinting in his praise for their project, and Judith's spirits soared. Life, which had been so dull and dreary for so many weeks was suddenly rich and full of promise. She had never been so happy.

Over the next few weeks, Mr. Mardale was a constant visitor to Greyfells, and a delightful companion as he escorted the ladies for walks over the fells, with the boys running at their side, whooping and laughing, but easily controlled by the tall young man.

Mr. Carrock had ridden out once again on one of his many business trips and Judith spared him little thought until Françoise called to see her one afternoon.

"You are so busee, Judith," she complained. "I do not see you, yet soon I go to London and I go with sad heart if I do not have talk weeth you."

Judith was touched. "But how nice of you, Françoise," she said warmly. "I did not realise you valued my friendship so much."

"You go always weeth Monsieur Mardale," said Françoise, pouting. "I am ver' cross weeth you."

"But . . . " Judith's warm smile faded a little. "He is a friend, and a neighbour."

"Ees not my dearest Aidan a neighbour and does not he weesh to be more than a good frien'?" asked Françoise. "You are stupeed, Judith. You do not see what would be so right for you, *and* for Mees Bess."

Judith's smile had completely vanished. Françoise was hardly discreet in her choice of words at times. At first she had excused the French girl, believing her use of English to be at fault, but now she knew Françoise better and she knew that she was inclined to speak her mind, either in English or French, however badly it was received.

"Surely that is my affair, Françoise," she said, rather coldly. "I do not wish to discuss Mr. Carrock, *or* Mr. Mardale."

"And you do not thank me when

I work so hard for you. My dearest Aidan needs a wife, and you need a husban' to take care of you and earn much monies for you. I tell him what beauty you have and he say it is so. You are beautiful. Here the pretty young lady is admired, but in Martinique, everyone would admire you and see your great beauty, and I remind Aidan, and he say it is so. He will have you for a wife. Then you say you will not have him for a husban'. Why not? Because you admire Monsieur Mardale who is beau to Mees Bess. Let Mees Bess marry Monsieur Mardale, and you will have Aidan and be my sister . . . no?"

"No!" cried Judith, scandalized. Was that *really* why Mr. Carrock had offered for her? Françoise had put him up to it! Set amidst a bevy of native girls in the West Indies, she would be in looks! Judith had never heard anything so preposterous in her life. Sometimes she thought that Françoise must be a little strange in her head!

And to suggest that Mr. Mardale should marry Bess! She wanted to laugh at the idea, but she was much too angry with Françoise. The French girl saw blue sparks in Judith's eyes, and she shrugged.

"So you are angry with me. Ah well, Judith, I have tried to do my best for you. Perhaps I make a mistake. Perhaps, after all, you are ordinary woman with ordinary mind, and not right for my dear Aidan. He deserves the best, does he not? Soon I go to London, and perhaps I see you before I go, perhaps not. I am sorree I have offended you."

Judith forced back her rage and managed to smile. "It is nothing, Françoise. I shall miss you."

"I, too. We could have been good frien's, and ver' good sisters. Me, I see it all like crystal, but you see through glass darkly. When you see crystal, it will be too late."

Judith laughed. Françoise was very droll at times. She watched the French

166

girl go regretfully. There would be many changes around her very soon, and she did not always welcome change. There would be new boys to teach. She was seeing Mrs. Laird who had a few more contacts for her, and together they would discuss these prospective pupils.

But meanwhile Mr. Mardale would be arriving shortly to take tea with her and Bess, and Judith's spirits soared once more. His presence at Hazlemont had certainly made the world a more delightful place for her and Bess.

* * *

He arrived a few minutes later and was welcomed with open delight by Judith and Bess, though sometimes Nanny Sherman shook her head a little as she set out a tray of tea and biscuits. The young gentleman certainly made himself at home and none could say that he was not a very fine young man, and very pleasant, but Nanny would have liked to know where it would all end.

Judith poured tea as usual and told Mr. Mardale that, sadly, their pupils only had a few more days before returning to their own homes.

"It was an experiment, but I feel it has been a success," she said, with satisfaction, "but I shall miss the boys. I have grown very fond of all three. Would you care for more tea, Mr. Mardale?"

She poured the tea from the large silver teapot and was about to pass it over to him when she looked up suddenly and her eyes were rivetted on a scene which shook her to the very foundations of her newfound happiness.

Mr. Mardale had turned to speak to Bess and as she replied shyly, their eyes met and Judith could see that they were oblivious to all else but themselves. Bess had never looked more beautiful as she gazed with naked adoration at Mr. Mardale, and he, too, was caught in a web which was binding them together with so much strength that they were powerless to resist it.

A wave of anger and hurt swept over Judith. Why should Bess take Mr. Mardale away from her? It was *she* to whom he had been attracted before Bess came on the scene. She had always worked hard for her sister and had tried to give her everything she needed in life. She had never before wanted anything for herself.

But now she wanted Mr. Mardale. She had never been in love before, but the pain in her heart was forcing her to accept that she loved Mr. Mardale more than she had ever loved anyone. And she had been so sure that he was beginning to return that love.

She wanted to hide her face and moan with pain against the knowledge that it was Bess to whom he was turning, but with a great effort, she forced herself to smile as he turned back to her and thanked her for the tea. He must not ever guess how stupid and vulnerable she had been.

His look was almost sightless as he accepted the cup and once again he turned to Bess.

"Would . . . would you do me the honour of paying a visit to Hazlemont for tea on Sunday afternoon?" he asked, somewhat hoarsely. "I am sure my grandparents would like to make your acquaintance since I have already told them so much about you, Miss Elizabeth . . . that is, *both* of you, of course, Miss Taverner," he added, hastily, the ready colour in his cheeks. "I would be happy to call at three o'clock for . . . for both of you, and to return you to Greyfells at whatever time you wish."

"I regret that I already have an appointment . . . with Mrs. Laird, wife of the Vicar," said Judith. "We are to discuss the new pupils."

Bess's face fell with disappointment.

"Oh, Judith, cannot you postpone that appointment with Mrs. Laird?" she asked.

Mr. Mardale's attitude also entreated her to reconsider. Judith swallowed and forced herself to make the bravest decision she had ever made.

"Since you wish my sister to pay a visit to your grandmother . . . your grandparents . . . Mr. Mardale, then I will consent to her accompanying you on Sunday afternoon. I am sure you will take good care of Bess and return her to Greyfells at a suitable hour."

Bess's eyes were like stars and Mr. Mardale also expressed his pleasure, but Judith could see now that the pleasure was merely his way of showing natural good manners, and meant nothing more than interest and, no doubt, liking. It was Bess who held all his attention.

"I will indeed take care of Miss Bess, Miss Taverner," he assured her eagerly. "I will see that she is returned home safely and in good heart."

Judith sighed a little. Suddenly she felt old; she felt older, even, than Mr. Mardale yet he must be her senior by at least four years. For a brief moment, she, herself, had been a very young girl, ready to fall in love and so sure that her beloved would return that love in full measure, but now she was the quiet, older sister to whom deference must be paid, and promises made that all would be proper for Bess.

Bess! The jealousy which had threatened to overwhelm Judith died away. It had all been a dream. She was glad she had not shown her heart to anyone, but had nursed her feelings to herself. No one would ever know how much it had hurt.

But there she was very wrong.

12

JUDITH informed her young pupils the following day that their parents would be coming to collect them as soon as they could conveniently do so.

"I expect your parents on Saturday evening," she told Matthew Dickson. "They wish to stay in Keswick for a few days. Mr. and Mrs. Forsyth hope to arrive here on Sunday morning. I am sure you must all be delighted to be going home again, and I think you must all feel much fitter and stronger than you did when you first arrived. Matthew, your cold has surely vanished completely, and Sam and Peter are quite as tall as Matthew now, with fine strong legs and brown arms. You will be equal to any boy of your age when you return home . . . "

"Miss Judith!"

Sam spoke up anxiously.

"Yes, Sam?"

"Am I as strong as a poor boy who lives in India. Am I as strong as the boys who live around the bazaars and look after themselves?"

"I should say you are a great deal stronger," said Judith, stoutly. "You eat well and sleep well. Some poor boys never get quite enough nourishment, and do not have such nice beds, all to themselves, as you do. I only hope your basic learning has also been good, but I have laid out samples of your work to show your parents and I am sure they will be very pleased with you. Now, Nanny has something special for your tea. You must all three have your hands washed before tea."

Sam hardly heard her. He went over to the low casement window and leaned his knee on the window seat, staring out at the scene which he had come to love so much. So often he had watched the changing colours of the mountains, according to the caprices of the weather, and in his young imagination the Himalayas could not be more beautiful or more grand. Far away he could see the sparkle of Bassenthwaite Lake, and the tiny, white-painted farmhouses where the herds of cattle were tended daily.

On the other side of Greyfells, the home grounds led on to the meadow ... the rough field which Judith had refused to sell ... and thence to the higher ground which must be as high as those mountains in the far distance. Sam could not bear to part with these great high fells when he returned once again to Manchester. Peter and Matthew had become firm friends and had played games together, kicking at a ball (and one another's shins) and playing with large chestnuts on a piece of string which Nanny Sherman had found for them in a kitchen drawer.

"You need fresh ones," she had said, "but you will be back in your own beds long afore the tree gives up its fruits."

The thought had chilled Sam's heart then, even though he had not cared about the chestnuts. He did not like the game which Matthew and Peter played with such enthusiasm. Sam loved his parents and wanted to see them again, but he also wanted to live in the mountains for a short while, even as the bazaar boys lived in India; those without parental supervision, and able to live by their wits. He could secrete some food from that which Nanny Sherman served up, and he could take warmer clothing lest it grew cold in the night. The bracken would make a fine bed, and for a little while he would be able to live amidst all the animals he loved so much. He had a strange inner craving to lie close to the warm earth, before he was torn away from it for ever. He could pretend he was also a rich boy, riding out to find wild animals, but he would never shoot them, and he would never want to be looked after by so many servants. He wanted to go alone.

Nanny Sherman came to find Judith on Saturday morning, and her eyes were wide with anxiety. She had Peter and Matthew on either side of her and they, too, were subdued and afraid.

"It's that Sam," said Nanny, "he has made off somewheres and he has not come back. These two stupid boys say he went late last night after I tucked them up, and they did not come to tell me. Did you ever hear the like of it, Miss Judith?"

Judith went pale. She had been trying to come to terms with her depression because the future did not beckon quite so brightly as she had expected. Now Nanny was delivering one more thing for her to worry about.

"*Where* has he gone?" she asked. "Don't either of you know? Didn't he tell you?"

Both boys looked at her silently.

"We do not know," said Peter. "He wants to live like an Indian boy,

177

and look after himself, just like Mr. Mardale told us. And he wants to live like a rich boy, too, and hunt wild animals, though Sam says he could not be cruel and kill them. He does not think anyone should kill animals."

"More like they'll kill him!" said Nanny in a dreadful voice, and both boys stared at her with frightened eyes, and Peter began to howl. Matthew followed in sympathy.

"Be quiet, Nanny," said Judith exasperated, "and you two stop crying. Where is Miss Bess?"

"Making curl cloths for her hair before she goes stepping out with the young gentleman," said Nanny.

"Wait here!" said Judith. "Do not move until I have a word with Miss Bess, then if she does not know anything, you two will tell me everything Sam has talked about recently . . . everything! Now do stop crying and *think* about it, so that you can tell me when I come back."

Their tears subsided now that they had been set a task.

* * *

Bess sang quietly to herself as she tore up strips of rags and wound them round her hair to form long sausage curls. She knew very well the purpose of her visit to Hazlemont. Jonathan wished her to meet his grandparents in lieu of his parents, then if all seemed to be well between them, he would wish to speak to Judith on her behalf, and Bess had no doubt that Judith would be happy to consent to a betrothal between herself and Jonathan Mardale.

Bess looked slightly more thoughtful. At one time she had been concerned because it seemed that Judith had also admired Mr. Mardale, but it had only been the natural admiration of a lady for a man so superior in charm and intellect. Judith's admiration had not ripened into anything more than that so that Bess's own joy and happiness lay in a future of such brightness and possibilities that her heart felt like to burst when she contemplated its every aspect. Hazlemont would belong to Jonathan's parents one day, but he was sure that they would wish to remain in India, and Jonathan would be asked to manage the estate. What could be better? He now had no wish to return to India and serve the Raj. He was perfectly content to remain at Hazlemont.

Judith had been right in thinking that an ideal match would be to someone who was a close neighbour. How terrible if that had been Mr. Carrock! She did not blame Judith for refusing that gentleman! If only he had Mr. Mardale's sensibilities, then that would, indeed, have been perfect and Judith might have accepted him after all. But then, of course, if Mr. Carrock had been as personable as Mr. Mardale, then he would not have offered for Judith. No doubt he had already tried some of the other eligible young ladies, but they had demurred when it came to the point and had backed off.

Suddenly the door of Bess' room flew open and Judith was there, her appearance almost wild with agitation. Bess' heart jumped with fright.

"What . . . ?" she began.

"Have you seen Sam?" asked Judith.

"Oh dear, how you startled me!" said Bess, much relieved. There was no bad news from Jonathan Mardale, as she had feared when she saw her sister's face.

"Sam?" she repeated. "Surely this is the morning of play for the boys."

"He is not in his room and has been absent all night. Has he ever said anything to you about going out at night?"

Bess's fingers stopped playing with her next piece of curler rag. This was rather more serious.

"Out all night? Oh dear. You . . . you mean he has run away?"

"He is living like an Indian boy, or

so I understand," said Judith, crisply. "He is savouring the delights of looking after himself as a poor boy, yet hunting wild creatures as though he were also the son of a maharajah. *Your* Mr. Mardale's talks on India have been rather too impressive for a boy like Sam."

"That is unfair!" cried Bess, leaping to her feet. "*You* approved of all he had to say and you enjoyed every word of it. You cannot blame Mr. Mardale if Sam takes his talk literally."

"You had better put a shawl over your hair," said Judith. "I need everyone to help . . . you, Nanny, Joss and our maidservants from the village. Do you not realise? Matthew's parents will arrive today and Mr. and Mrs. Forsyth will be here tomorrow morning. What will happen if they find that Sam is missing?"

Bess turned pale. "Perhaps we ought to get Mr. Mardale to help," she suggested, but Judith had already hurried from the room.

Life had become a nightmare for Judith once more. From the heights of her great happiness when she had thought that Mr. Mardale returned her admiration in full measure, she sank to the depths of despair. Why had she ever believed herself capable of being in charge of three young boys who were likely to behave irrationally? She had no knowledge whatsoever of the ideals and inspirations of a male child, and it had never for one moment occurred to her that one of her three charges might take Mr. Mardale's lecture on India so literally that he would try to live that life for himself! How could he *think* to translate the life of a boy in that far off country to life close to Greyfells! Judith marvelled that Sam could be so . . . so impressionable!

She threw on her oldest dark brown cloak and changed her shoes for a pair of heavy boots. They looked ridiculous with her pretty cotton gown (another of her mother's) but she did not care.

"He might have gone towards the rough shoot and the fells," she said to Nanny. "You know how he loves the meadow. Peter says he was always talking about the Himalayas, however. Perhaps his imagination will have built up the fells into great mountainous peaks. I think we should find Joss and ask him to inform Mr. Mardale. Perhaps he would be good enough to organize a search party. Oh, Nanny, if we do not find him . . . we . . . I . . . I will inform the Reverend Stephen Laird who will get in touch with Sam's parents. On, Nanny, how can I ever *look* at Sam's parents, if I have lost him? They love him so much and truth to tell, so do I!"

"Me, too, Miss Judith," said Nanny, whose red-rimmed frightened eyes told their own tale.

But Judith's fears were, as yet, too deep even for tears and she set off towards the rough shoot meadow with her heart pounding in her ribs. Nanny had handed her a bag containing a small flask of brandy and bandages in case the child was wounded, and she carried a stout stick to keep any animal at bay. For the most part the wild creatures were shy of Man, but if Sam lay wounded on the fells, might that not attract the attention of some fierce creature?

Calling his name repeatedly, Judith paused to peer into every crevice and behind every boulder. It was only when she neared the land which belonged to Burroughs Park that her footsteps faltered, then she began to run as she heard the sound of men's voices, and realised that she was nearing the location of Mr. Carrock's new lead mine.

Two men, one right-handed and one left-handed worked side by side striking the drills, which they called jumpers, so that they bored parallel holes into the hard rock, and suddenly Judith began to remember, with chilling clarity, fragments of information she had picked up from Joss, who might have been tempted to ask for work as a miner had he not owed loyalty to Miss Judith.

"They've got gunpowder in from Elterwater Powder Works, Miss Judith," said Joss. "I saw the powder cart bringing it up to the mine. They had several big twenty-five pound wooden casks. Thomas Casson and John Fletcher are working together wi' the jumpers, Miss Judith. Thomas Casson is left-handed and he gets paid more. Two men do better on hard rock than double-hand men and they are always looking for left-handed men and they get paid more, Miss Judith."

She had scarcely been listening. At the time her head had been full of dreams of Mr. Mardale.

"*I'm* left-handed, Miss Judith," Joss had said, wistfully, and she had come out of her dreams and had briskly discouraged him from trying to fill her head with useless information.

"That henhouse will have to be

repaired, Joss," she had said, severely, "else the fox will be away with more chickens. It is time for the vixen to train her young into new territory and I fancy that there is a fine young dog-fox in our vicinity. The hens have been restless, and the young lambs were bleating in the night. Do make sure of it, Joss."

"Aye, ma'am," said Joss dolefully.

He would have liked a try at hammering one of those jumpers, though most likely he would have been given the task of adding water to make the bores move faster. But it seemed like manly work to him, though John Fletcher said it was not so pleasant underground, especially if the ventilation and drainage were poor. In any case, he had better mend the henhouse. Miss Judith had a sharp tongue and a sharper eye for work badly done. She was worse than a man to work for, because he found himself doing much more for her, since she was a young lady.

Now Judith was remembering her conversation with Joss with greater and greater clarity. Suppose ... suppose some of that gunpowder was going to be used now. Suppose that Sam was in the area, and could not hear any warning shouts. It would be very dangerous for him.

Judith tried to shout as she stumbled forward, but something seemed to have happened to her vocal chords. She could not make herself heard. Her voice sounded like rough croaking in her own ears.

She could see the men working quite clearly, but the sound of hammer blows seemed to drown out her feeble efforts at attracting attention.

One man in dark clothing looked round and she waved her hand, then threw off her cloak, hoping that the brighter colour of her gown would show up against the landscape better than her dark cloak. For good measure she held up her skirts and waved her petticoats, which were white. In such dire necessity there was no room for modesty.

Then suddenly her heavy boot caught on an outcrop of rock, and Judith fell heavily. For a moment she lay winded, dimly aware that the hammering had not stopped, then a great pain shot up her leg and she felt very sick as she tried to raise herself, and to try one more time to attract attention.

She held on to the rough grasses then the ground began to whirl about her and everything became black.

13

SOMETHING was still hammering loudly in Judith's head when she came to herself once more, and her mouth felt dry and parched.

"Her eyes open themselves," said Françoise, bending over her.

"Water," whispered Judith.

"She will be seeck," said Françoise. "She needs the herb tea to make her sleep again, then she will feel better. Maman will help. She is ver' good nurse."

A cup was held to Judith's lips and she drank greedily, then she felt very sick indeed.

"Where am I?" she asked.

"You are safe, my Judith," said Françoise, happily. "You are here, at Burroughs Park. Dearest Aidan brought you home."

Remembrance was returning, and

with it Judith's brain seemed to be in a fever.

"Sam!" she cried, and Madame de Ridieux pressed something soothing on to her forehead.

"Rest easy," she said in French. "Rest easy, little one."

"Sam ees safe. He ees fed and bathed by Nanny Sherman, and is now at Greyfells. Aidan has gone there, too. Sam's parents come for him, also the little Peter. Matthew, too. They all go home."

The enormous relief of it made Judith's body tremble like a leaf. She was aware that her right leg was bandaged and that it was causing her great pain, but that was bearable after all the pain and agony of believing she had lost Sam.

"Where was he?" she asked.

"He had been on the rough ground where you were searching, then he lost his way and wandered close to Hazlemont," said Françoise. "Mr. Mardale found him. He take him to

Greyfells and to Mees Bess. They arrange everything together. No need for worry."

A coloured woman had come into the room, bearing a hot jar covered with a cloth, and this she put into Judith's bed. She, too, spoke French with an unusual accent, and Judith was grateful for the warmth on her shivering body. The coloured woman, whom Françoise named Chloe, held a warm drink to her lips and she drank it without protest.

"There, the little one will sleep again," Madame de Ridieux said, with satisfaction.

"Dearest Aidan is very angry."

Françoise's clear voice came to Judith through clouds of darkness. "He weel not rest until it is all as he weeshes. Poor Judith . . ."

Again she slept and when she woke again it was night and only Chloe was in her room. The coloured woman wore a large white apron and she was dozing in a chair which had been pulled up to the fire.

As Judith made a small sound, she was immediately awake, and in the semi-darkness of the room, she made Judith comfortable so that once against she slept. When she finally awoke, the sun shone into a room bright with colour. The wallpaper was dainty with tiny sprigs of pink roses intermingled with trailing blue ribbons, and fresh white curtains, which matched her bedcovers, billowed gently at an open window.

Judith pulled herself up on her pillows, wincing at the pain in her leg. She wore a pretty gown with white lace at the neck and wrists, but as she moved, her leg grew more and more painful so that she cried out a little. Immediately Françoise ran into the room.

"Ah, you are awake," she cried with delight, "and you are so much better. That is good. Aidan is waiting to see you when you are better."

"What happened? Why am I here?" Judith asked.

Françoise's eyes widened. "You do not remember? You had a fall near to the new lead mines which Aidan is developing. You were looking for the leetle boy, Sam."

Judith swallowed. She was remembering very well. She had lost Sam, but he had been returned to his parents. Had Françoise said that Mr. Carrock had seen Sam's parents and that he, Mr. Carrock, was very angry?

She threw back the bedclothes.

"I must rise," she told Françoise. "Where is my clothing? I must return to Greyfells without delay."

"Ah, non, non!" cried Françoise "it is not possible! You have been ill. You have had to sleep for three days and you have been bad in your head. All is well at Greyfells. Aidan is attending to everything for you. There is no worry for you at all. The old one . . . Nanny Sherman . . . looks after Mees Bess and Aidan sends servants to help the good

Joss and the maidservants."

"The boys . . . "

"They have gone. You have forgotten that I have told you they are all well, and have gone to their parents. You mus' rest because your leg is very bad, but Chloe will mend it for you. First you have breakfast, then I weel make you pretty for dearest Aidan. That is good. You must be hungry."

Surprisingly Judith was hungry, even if the thought of the coming interview with Aidan Carrock was taking away her good appetite. He had every right to be angry with her on behalf of the parents of her boys. She should never have taken on such a task. She was not competent to do such a thing.

Then there was Mr. Mardale. He had found Sam for her, or to be more correct, for Bess. It was Bess who was Mr. Mardale's primary consideration. Life held out very fine promise for her sister and Judith offered a silent prayer of thanks to God for this. For a little while she must have been mad to be so jealous of Bess, but she could not tear Mr. Mardale out of her own heart so quickly.

As she ate her breakfast, she thought about his handsome looks and fine profile. Whatever Françoise said about her own looks, she knew now that she was a plain woman. It was Bess who had the beauty. She would have to resign herself to the fact that she had neither beauty nor money. Yet what was she going to do with her life now? How could she advertise for more pupils when she no longer felt competent to deal with them? How could she look after six small boys, when she could not even control three? Besides, Mr. Mardale might offer for Bess and she could not run a school single-handed, and with the loss of her investments, her income would be much too small to keep up Greyfells, even if she were alone.

"You are very solemn," said Françoise as she insisted upon gently brushing Judith's hair into long dark brown curls which tumbled about her shoulders. "Are you in great pain, poor Judith?"

"A little," Judith admitted.

"Poor little one. I will be queeck. But I want you to look so beautiful for dearest Aidan, even if you feel seeck."

In order that his anger against her should cool? wondered Judith. If her beauty was meant to influence his temper, then the coming interview would no doubt be stormy indeed!

The coloured maidservant, Chloe, had washed her gently but thoroughly, and Françoise had found another frothy bedgown for her to wear which, she informed Judith, had been part of her trousseau.

"You are being very kind to me, Françoise," Judith said gratefully. "I . . . I don't know why you should be so kind. I mean . . . I have never forgotten that I was so rude to you when we first met. I . . . I am so often ashamed of that, but I want you to know that I am most grateful to you for being so nice to me. You could so easily have turned a cold shoulder."

"That ees forgotten. It amused me. It is I who should apologise to you because we played treecks, Aidan and I, and it was *my* fault. It was *my* idea after the ladies with the beeg crocodile teeth came calling with their daughters . . . poor little ones. Lambs who are at the slaughter, though dear Aidan would be kind to any of those lambs. But not to the mamas . . . non! So you see, I have tried to make amends to you, but soon I did so because I love you for yourself. Soon I see how it is with you and I admire you ver' much. We are frien's now."

"We are friends," said Judith, and allowed Françoise to fasten a ribbon in her hair. She felt clean and fresh, but she would have preferred to be on her feet and fully gowned before she met Mr. Carrock again.

He walked into her bedroom half an hour later, asking that Chloe should remain.

"She speaks no English," said Mr. Carrock, as he sat down beside Judith's bed. "We can converse freely, but she will be at hand should you need the help of a woman. Are you in great pain, Miss Judith?"

"It is much better," she said, pulling up her bed covers.

"I shall not tire you, if I can help it."

"I . . . I am sorry," she apologised. "I should never have allowed the boys to run on the rough fell. I can see that it would have been dangerous for them. I know Sam was found near Hazlemont, but he had been on the fells and he could easily have explored the mine workings. I could not believe that he would run away when he was not supervised. I thought . . . I thought they were all happy at Greyfells."

"He was *very* happy at Greyfells," said Mr. Carrock, rather drily. "I understand that the object of his exercise was to gain a little more of Greyfells for himself. He did not want to return home to Manchester. He loves the mountains. You will be happy to hear that his parents intend to buy a small property somewhere in the Lake District so that the twins can spend every summer in the good mountain air. They are very pleased to have lost their 'delicate' boys, and to have gained a pair of young ruffians. The same can be said for young Matthew."

Judith's face lit up.

"You mean they are happy with what I have done?"

"Very happy."

Again Mr. Carrock's voice was dry. He reached into his pocket and brought out a purse of coins, which he placed beside her bed. "There is a sum of money which represents a bonus for you."

"A . . . a bonus?" she asked.

"I ascertained the exact amount of money which you charged for educating and restoring those children to full health. It would barely have covered half of the meals which Nanny Sherman cooked for them. I put it to the parents that it may have been sufficient to feed delicate boys, but that the boys had ceased to be delicate after a fairly short period of time, and that their appetites had correspondingly improved beyond all measure. They are both wealthy families. They can afford to pay a great deal more for the services you have rendered their children. You have restored youngsters to glowing health which no bottled tonics in the world could have done. I suggested a proper recompense and the parents were happy to agree."

Judith's face had flushed rosily.

"But . . . but I shall have been paid *very* well indeed, with a bonus," she said, and as she looked at the gold coins, her eyes returned to him wonderingly.

"I hardly know what to say, Mr. Carrock. This will make a great difference to my situation. Yet I feel that I do not deserve it. I . . . I cannot predict what a boy is going to do. I do not understand their minds. Mr. Mardale talked to them about life in India and it was very impressive. I did not realise how impressive it would be on young minds."

Her eyes were full of thought, and he watched her keenly.

"Ah yes ... Mardale ... " he repeated. "He had been filling up their heads ... "

"It was a very fine lecture," she said, swiftly. "The boys ... we *all* enjoyed it."

Again he looked at her keenly, then he sighed.

"I am quite sure you all found it very fascinating, Miss Judith," he said, heavily. "Mardale is, after all, a ... a fine chap." He could say little else. Mardale was a fine fellow.

"I had intended to advertise for more pupils, with the help of the Reverend and Mrs. Laird, if the parents of my boys were satisfied," said Judith. "Now, well, I hardly know what to do."

"You will be in bed for at least two

weeks," said Mr. Carrock. "The doctor insists. After which you will have to rest your leg for a further two weeks."

"Four whole weeks!" cried Judith "Oh no, Mr. Carrock, I cannot lie a-bed for four whole weeks. There is too much to do."

He lifted the bag and clinked it.

"You are not penniless, Miss Judith."

"But there is always work to be done in order to earn money for the future. You do not understand, Mr. Carrock. Joss must be supervised and I must also see that any waste food from the kitchen is put to feeding the animals. And the maidservants grow lax if one does not check on their work, and I must be sure that the henhouse is safe against the fox. Joss might forget to mend it."

Mr. Carrock's eyes hardened again.

"It is not fitting that these worries should be on your shoulders," he said, sternly. "You will not help yourself by refusing to rest, Miss Judith, but in any case, there is no need for you to worry further. Surely you can see by now that the best solution is for you to accept my proposal of marriage, and I will arrange to have Greyfells looked after by a manager, and administer the property with my own. Your sister can remain there until . . . until she, herself, marries then other arrangements can be made. It is not fitting for Miss Bess to be married before you. In fact, it is not fitting that you have no older relative, male or female, to look after your interests a little better."

He turned away almost angrily and she flushed as she looked at him. Why was he offering for her? She did not believe that Françoise had merely influenced him into choosing her. He could marry anyone in the county! Was he so altruistic that he would offer for *her* rather than a girl already well-endowed with everything she could want, merely because he felt that she, Judith, was in want of care and protection? She wanted to tell him, proudly, that she was perfectly capable of managing her own affairs. But she could not. Had not she proved to the world that she was completely incapable of managing her own affairs?

It would be so easy to say that she would marry Mr. Carrock, but although she had known for many years what marriage would mean (no countrywoman who had had to help in the care of animals was ever ignorant), it was a frightening prospect when one met such a proposal face to face. She would have to live in very close harmony with this man, and she was not sure that she even liked him! She thought about Mr. Mardale, but remembered again that it was Bess whom he wanted, and she felt like weeping for the pain of such knowledge.

Mr. Carrock's eyes had never left her face. His mouth twisted when he saw the hint of tears in her eyes, quickly suppressed. He knew she was attracted to Mardale.

"I shall not expect love from you," he said, brusquely, "but I shall expect you to *respect* me, and to respect my wishes. I would also expect your loyalty to me, and my family. I should want . . . " he paused, " . . . I should want a family. Let us be quite clear about that. In return I would respect your privacy, when you wish it. Your family and those who depend upon you would want for nothing. Your estate would be administered along with my own and would not be allowed to deteriorate." He listed an exceedingly well-informed number of repairs which required to be carried out. "These would all be undertaken."

"Why are you doing this?" she asked.

He looked taken aback and for a brief moment there was something between them which she could not quite grasp. His eyes seemed to hold hers until she tried to back away from something which made her feel afraid, yet caught and held her at the same time.

"I told you," he said, softly. "I need

a wife. You are as well-born as any young lady I have met and it would be more expedient for me to marry you than . . . than any other young woman in the vicinity. As to love . . . " He shrugged and smiled a little. " . . . we need not concern ourselves with that, if you do not feel you . . . " again his voice dropped almost to a whisper, " . . . feel you could love me."

"May I think it over?" she asked.

He rose to his feet. "No, you may not. It is some time since I first proposed marriage to you. You have had ample time to think it over. If you agree, I shall arrange with the Reverend Stephen Laird to marry us here at Burroughs Park. It is better that you should rest here as my wife, then I shall be able to handle your affairs the more easily. It will be a quiet wedding, but your sister can act as bridesmaid. Françoise and her mother will arrange it. Soon they will have to return to London so it is better that you should be married to me before

Françoise leaves Burroughs Park."

"It is all a matter of expediency," said Judith, wearily.

He was quite correct. It was the most sensible solution to her future and she had never *truly* expected to marry for love. She ought to thank him for offering for her in the first place, but something in her prevented her from meekly bowing to the dictates of Mr. Carrock.

I shall quarrel with him, she thought. I shall not be a meek wife for him to order about.

Before she could stop herself, she had put these points to Mr. Carrock, and he threw back his head and laughed.

"If you quarrel too much with me, I shall beat you," he promised. "That I promise you. Do you still accept?"

"I accept," she said, huskily and he turned away from her for a long moment. When he looked at her again, his face was calm.

"I shall arrange everything," he said. "My sister-in-law calls me Aidan. I would like you to do so."

"Very well . . . Aidan."

He picked up her hand, and swiftly kissed her fingers.

"I will bring your sister to see you," he said. "With your permission, I will tell Elizabeth about our new relationship."

Again Judith agreed. Her fingers felt warm from his lips and her heart also felt warm and at peace. She wondered what Bess would say. Her sister had only paid quick visits to see her at Burroughs Park, and she had been too fatigued to talk with her at any great length. But she felt much better now, and longed to see Bess, and Nanny.

"I will send Françoise to you, my dear," said Aidan, and walked out of the room.

14

THE next few days took on a dreamlike quality for Judith. Bess called to see her and informed her that Mr. Carrock had made new arrangements for the care of Greyfells, and that more maidservants were being employed in the house, with strong men to help Joss. Much needed repairs to the house and out-buildings were now under way.

"Mrs. Françoise Carrock has also called." she said, rather formally. Burroughs Park always made her feel very nervous and rather over-awed by its size and magnificence. "She has ordered the dressmaker. She says I must have a new gown because I am expected to be bridesmaid to you, Judith. It is very exciting. Also . . . " she blushed prettily, " . . . also Mr. Mardale desires to see you to discuss my future happiness, but Mr. Carrock has said that all must wait until after you are married. Thereafter he will take all such responsibilities on his shoulders. How strange it is that our household is now being arranged from Burroughs Park, and all to Mr. Carrock's liking, I hope you are happy, Judith," she added, biting her lip nervously, "because he is a very strong, self-willed man and he does not like to be crossed. Mr. Mardale does not find him very co-operative."

Judith sat up in bed. She frowned a little and some of the relief and relaxation which had settled upon her began to evaporate. It had been very pleasant to lie in this soft bed at Burroughs Park and allow Aidan Carrock to take charge of her responsibilities, and for a few days she had been too tired to worry about her own affairs, but with Bess's visit, her artless words seemed to drop like a sprinkling of icy water over Judith's head.

"The dressmaker!" she repeated.

"We cannot afford the dressmaker."

"Mr. Carrock is arranging everything," said Bess, "and Françoise says your gown is to be of the finest quality and most elegant style and it will be made in London. She desired your measurements."

Judith sat up even straighter, then winced with the pain in her leg. It was a little better but still caused great discomfort. Françoise had called to see her and had chattered a great deal, using a mixture of French and English. She had mentioned something about a special gown, but Judith had been too relaxed to listen properly. She had allowed her mind to wander and Françoise's words had had little meaning for her.

"The wedding is going to be very quiet," she told Bess. "I shall wear a simple gown. You must have misunderstood Françoise."

She could hardly understand why Bess's words had irritated her, then slowly she began to assimilate all she had heard. Mr. Mardale was offering for Bess, and Aidan Carrock was going to make himself responsible for her sister's future when he became her husband. And surely he must consider Mr. Mardale a most suitable husband for Bess.

Judith looked at her sister. Bess's eyes glowed, now that she had got over her nerves, and she was in excellent looks. How happy she must be to be marrying a man she obviously loved so much. How wonderful marriage must be under such circumstances. Once more her leg felt painful and depression settled upon her.

"I think I am a little tired, Bess," she said. "I'll rest now."

Bess stared at her rather wonderingly.

"I cannot believe that he will be my brother," she said.

And I cannot believe, thought Judith silently, that he is going to be my husband! Certainly she could not allow Aidan to pay for a bridesmaid's gown for Bess and she would rather be married in a bed-gown than have him pay for a bridal gown for herself.

She closed her eyes and Bess rose, then dropped a kiss on her cheek.

"How well things are turning out for us," she said, happily. "I will tell Nanny that you are in good spirits."

* * *

Aidan called to see her an hour later and his smile faded when he saw the brooding look in her eyes as he bent to take her hand.

"I would have thought to see you greatly cheered by your sister's visit," he said. "Surely I have removed all worries which might have retarded your recovery, Judith. I would have thought she had set your mind at rest with regard to Greyfells."

"She told me of your administrations," Judith said, "and there are some things which I do not consider very proper. My sister's bridesmaid's gown must be paid for by myself, also the bridal gown which I understand Françoise has commissioned for me. I did not understand that she meant to arrange for very special gowns to be made. After all, it is a very quiet wedding, and I would wish to have gowns made which I can afford."

He was frowning. "The cost of your gown is as nothing. You are my affianced wife, and I see no reason why I cannot pay for your gowns. This a trifling matter. I have been busy on our account . . . "

"*Affianced* wife," she interrupted. "We are not married yet, sir."

His lips firmed and he drew in his breath impatiently.

"No, but I wish my bride and her sister to look fitting for such an occasion at Burroughs Park. I have decided to invite local people who will be our neighbours and, I hope, friends for the rest of our lives. I know you will have to sit at the ceremony and thereafter, my dear, but I think it is proper to have a wedding which is witnessed by a reasonable number of people. We will not have a shabby affair."

She ran a tongue over her lips, feeling suddenly nervous. A small quiet ceremony had not troubled her too greatly, but the thought of a grand affair was alarming. Why should he change his mind about this? She could see very well what Bess meant when she said he was taking over their affairs.

"I . . . I understand from my sister that . . . that Mr. Mardale wishes to . . . to consult me about my sister's future," she said painfully.

If Mr. Mardale was going to offer for Bess, surely she was entitled to be consulted and not have the matter postponed until after her marriage, then left to Aidan Carrock. This was probably the last thing she would be able to do for Bess, and she wanted to be responsible for that matter herself.

His eyes hardened.

"There is no need to concern yourself. I shall attend to Mardale. It is better that he should tell me his plans for his future, and that of his bride."

"No! I wish to see him myself," she said, firmly. "This is something which I wish to do *myself*."

He had been wandering round the room and now he came to stand beside the bed, looking down on her thoughtfully until his dark eyes began to glitter.

"Very well, it shall be as you wish. You should never have been left in such case. As I said before, I have been busy on behalf on our betrothal, and have brought this ring for you. I think we will find that it is the correct size, but it can be altered if it should prove necessary. It has been cleaned by our jeweller. You will be given other family jewels after you become my wife. But for now . . . "

He lifted up her left hand and examined it once more as he had done in the past, then slipped the most magnificent diamond she had ever seen on to her third finger.

Judith gasped as the diamond glowed with fire, reflecting all the colours of the spectrum. It seemed to burn with a life of its own.

Then he picked up the purse of coins which he had placed on the table by her bedside several days before.

"As to paying for your own gown and that of your bridesmaid, this will suffice since you wish to be so independent. And as to seeing Mardale, I will arrange for that, also, since you feel that the matter cannot wait. Though I promise you that if you have some fanciful idea that you can persuade him, even now, to choose the elder sister, whilst under *my* roof, you can forget such an idea. You have promised me, before witnesses, that you will be my wife, and I do not intend to let you go. And as for Mardale, he desires Miss Elizabeth. You had best make up your mind to it."

Judith gasped and wanted to deny that she had had any such idea with indignation. Yet was there not some

218

truth in it? In her most secret heart, hardly acknowledging the matter even to herself, was not this her dream?

He looked at her long and hard, as though he could see into her soul, and she thought that she saw contempt in his gaze. She flushed deeply and the heavy ring seemed to bite into her finger, reminding her that she was no longer free. She was tied to this man by her promise, and very soon she would be tied to him irrevocably.

"I . . . I did not think of such a thing, sir," she defended in a low voice.

"Then you will not be disappointed. The doctor says you may get up for a little and become used to sitting in a chair. Your leg will be rested on a footstool. He warns that it may pain you greatly, but it is now bad for you to remain a-bed all the time. Chloe will help you, and will make you as comfortable as possible."

Chloe had been walking in and out of her room while Aidan spoke with her. Now he turned and strode from the room, and she felt greatly at odds with herself. They would always quarrel, she thought unhappily. She did not face a very peaceful marriage. Why was he so determined to have her for a wife? She could not believe that it was merely because Françoise had pointed out the advantages of marrying his nearest neighbour!

Events moved so swiftly that Judith had no time to think too deeply about her situation. Madame de Ridieux and Françoise arranged the wedding and the house was kept very busy with all the preparations. Many people called to pay their respects and to leave wedding gifts, though Judith was only allowed the briefest contact with such acquaintances that she might not be too fatigued.

One who stayed longer was Mrs. Agnes Laird, who also seemed rather nervous of Burroughs Park, and who greeted Judith rather anxiously.

"I was so sorry to hear about your

accident, Miss Judith," she said, "and for such a reason! I was very cross with young Sam."

"It was entirely my own fault," said Judith.

"What a surprise to hear about your forthcoming marriage," she went on, then she bent forward. "Are you happy, my dear?" she asked, anxiously. "I know it is so much more suitable to be married than that you should teach delicate boys and improve their health as well as their minds, but . . . but I would like to see you very happy in your marriage. Mr. and Mrs. Forsyth, also the Dicksons, are delighted with the improvement in their sons, and the Vicar has been most happy with letters he has received. Each have contributed towards buying a new organ for the church. We can only say that your experiment, on our advice, was a great success."

"I am delighted," said Judith.

The days she had spent teaching, even though she had enjoyed the task were beginning to recede into the past and her main memory was of extreme anxiety over making ends meet. It would have been so easy to relax and think those days gone, yet some deep uneasiness still held her in thrall, and Mrs. Laird's eyes were concerned as she looked et Judith's pale face.

"I would like you to be happy," Mrs. Laird murmured, "but marriage is a very big step and is for the rest of your life, Miss Judith. If . . . if you want to change your mind . . . although I should not be talking to you like this, and only do so because you have no close woman relative, but if you want to change your mind, the Vicar and I could help, so do not hesitate to call on us."

"Why should I want to change my mind?" Judith asked, a trifle sharply.

Mrs. Laird looked exceedingly uncomfortable. "There have been rumours . . . "

"What sort of rumours?"

They could hear the light, pretty

voice of Françoise as she walked up the stairs, talking avidly to Madame de Ridieux.

Mrs. Laird sat back in her chair.

"They are not important," she said, quickly. "People gossip carelessly. The main thing is that you would hold a fine position in the neighbourhood. I think . . . " her eyes were considering, " . . . I think you would hold that position very well, Miss Judith."

Judith sighed. It would be like learning a whole new task, she thought. No wonder Mrs. Laird was anxious about her, and no doubt the rumours would be put about by people who considered her unfitted for the task. But she was to remember Mrs. Laird's words much later.

★ ★ ★

Mr. Mardale came to see her, and although they managed to speak privately together, Chloe was in the room and Aidan was also within call, walking up and down rather nervously, and glancing towards the chair by the window where Judith now sat each day.

"You are the head of the family, Miss Taverner," said Mr. Mardale, formally, "though I know that soon Mr. Carrock will be in full charge of your affairs. Meanwhile, I feel it would be more proper if I asked your permission to propose marriage to Miss Elizabeth. There will be many local people at the wedding. I would like it to be known that Miss Elizabeth is my affianced wife, and that our wedding will be arranged shortly. With your permission, it will be a quiet affair, but I feel that it would be expedient for us to be married very soon since Miss Elizabeth wishes to remain at Greyfells, rather than to move here to Burroughs Park. I feel that she will require protection . . . "

"I think Mr. Carrock wishes her to move here for a short while after the wedding, but I quite understand the position," said Judith, carefully. She looked up at Mr. Mardale who was a splendid figure in his dark green velvet riding coat. Bess was a lucky young woman.

"I have brought details of my financial position, but Mr. Carrock would be very pleased to look into these on your behalf and that of Miss Elizabeth. With your permission, that could be taken care of for you."

His eyes were anxious as he looked at her.

"I . . . I give my permission," she whispered and he seized her hand and kissed her fingers eagerly.

"I will always take care of her," he said, fervently. "I love her very much."

Judith's eyes were almost unseeing for a little while after he had gone, then she realised that Aidan stood beside her.

"So it is done," he said, rather harshly. "Does it make you happy to have taken on that responsibility for yourself? Are you still pleased with your own independence?"

She bit her lip. "It is the last thing I can do for my sister," she said, quietly, and suddenly his strong fingers were caressing her own.

"I wish I could make you a child again," he said, unexpectedly, and his voice was gentle. "I wish I could have known you when you were a little girl."

"Why?" she asked, surprised.

He shook his head as though unable to explain.

"Children sometimes have to be disappointed. Grown-ups, too, sometimes. There are some things I will never be able to give you."

"Such as?"

He dropped her hand and went to look out of the window. Together they could see the tall figure of Mr. Mardale as he went to collect his horse.

"Love," he said, softly. "One cannot take love out of a box and have it refurbished for you to wear, as one does a ring. Love cannot be manipulated, or manoeuvred. That is something I cannot do for you."

He turned abruptly and walked away from her and she began to twist the ring on her finger. It had been placed there without love. It was something she would have to learn to accept.

But, strangely, she no longer envied her sister because of Mr. Mardale. He was a fine young man, but he was not quite so handsome as she had believed. In fact, there were times, today, as they had talked together when he seemed almost ordinary.

But Bess and he belonged together, and she was happy for them both.

15

THEY were married a week later at Burroughs Park.

Françoise had supervised the purchase of Judith's wedding gown, and it was surely the most beautiful gown she had ever seen. It was made of the finest of white silk, richly embroidered with silver and trimmed with exquisite lace at the neck, sleeves and hemline where it had been caught up in small delicately-embroidered flowers. It was so beautiful that Judith thought it should have been made for a princess.

Françoise and Bess had also found Mrs. Taverner's wedding veil and this had been cleaned and refurbished so that both Françoise and Madame de Ridieux exclaimed with admiration and delight when Judith was dressed in her wedding finery. The dress emphasized Judith's splendid figure to perfection, the wide sweeping skirts hiding her leg which was still bandaged, and the veil softly draped over her dark curls and lovely sloping shoulders.

"It is true that you are indeed a great beauty," said Françoise, sighing. "I would be so jealous if it were not for my dearest Simon," she said, frankly. "When I first meet Aidan, I theenk I love him and he love me, and Papa say it is a good match. Then I meet Simon and he seem the older brother . . . He is such sobersides. But I love the sobersides. He has ver' important position for Government and such respect, and I love him. But I love Aidan still and want for him to be happy and today he will be happy with you."

Judith listened to her prattle with half an ear. Françoise seemed to love everybody. She supervised Bess as she, too, was gowned in the beautiful shell-pink creation which had been chosen for her, and Judith's eyes were bright as they rested on her sister. Her own looks had always taken second place, and her pride and admiration were all for Bess.

"You look very beautiful, sister," she said, warmly.

"But . . . but so do you," said Bess, almost wondering, "even better than when we went to the ball."

It was almost as though she were seeing Judith for the first time, and really appreciating her looks. Although she had been wholly satisfied with her own appearance, she could see now that she was of more ordinary beauty compared with the bride. Judith had always looked rather unusual, but, dressed in a beautiful gown, she looked like a wonderful painting.

"How is your leg?" she asked.

"Better. I shall be able to stand for the ceremony but I cannot walk around. It is a great nuisance."

Yet . . . was it? Aidan had said, with rather stiff courtesy, that she need not move from this guest room to the master bedroom until after she was quite well, and Judith hoped that her sigh of relief had not offended him too much. He had turned and left the room so abruptly that she could not decide.

"I am glad we are in good case," whispered Bess, as they waited to be conducted to the great hall where the ceremony would be performed. "Mr. Carrock has invited so many of our neighbouring families. I fear we will attract all eyes."

Judith's face, already pale, began to look very white, but when she was helped to the great hall, and placed on a gold velvet chair where she would rest before and after the ceremony, her colour returned and her heart beat loudly with nerves. Aidan stood beside her, looking tall and magnificent in burgundy velvet.

He had given her a reassuring smile and suddenly Judith felt her nerves and apprehension lessening. She was very much aware of the assembled guests and of the splendour of her own wedding, and there was pride in her heart. Many young ladies in her situation had married much older men, some of them widowers with a ready-made family almost as old as the bride. She should thank God that Aidan Carrock had taken her for a wife and accept her good fortune without further questioning.

Her leg was painful, but she managed to stand beside her bridegroom during the ceremony, and to make her vows in her firm, rich voice which drew reassuring pressure from Aidan's fingers, then soon she wore a plain band of gold on her finger beside the magnificent betrothal ring, and she was being wished happiness by her sister and Françoise, though she was barely conscious of more than Aidan's dark eyes and his tiny smile, almost of triumph.

Judith received many good wishes and compliments from the assembled guests and she was glad that Françoise had chosen this magnificent gown in the finest of silk for her to wear. It gave her confidence to receive all the compliments, gracefully.

Aidan remained by her side as she was once again helped into her chair. There was little opportunity for private conversation between them, but she was glad of the reassuring pressure of his fingers on her shoulder as he stood beside her. Then he was called away for consultation with regard to the magnificent refreshments which Madame de Ridieux had helped to organize.

For a short time Judith was on her own, and very glad of a respite. Then the voices of two ladies came to her clearly.

"But it *still* seems a trifle odd that he should choose Miss Taverner. Her looks are unusual, I grant you, but it is her sister who is the beauty."

"Ah, but Miss Taverner is the elder daughter and as such, she owns Greyfells, my dear, and besides she is not so likely to object to his . . . ah . . . fixation."

"I do not understand."

"Everyone knows, my dear, that he has always been in love with the French lady who married his brother. The French have strange ideas on love. They are very practical regarding marriage, then they feel free to love where they will. It is said *she* arranged the match. But of course, it is also expedient because of the mine. The wealthy mineral deposits do not lie towards Burroughs. They run towards Greyfells, and Miss Taverner would not sell her land. It will bring Mr. Carrock great wealth and my husband has heard there is zinc as well as lead. Miss Taverner . . . or should I say the new Mrs. Carrock? . . . is not a penniless girl . . . "

Judith had been unable to move and the voices had come to her quite clearly from behind a pillar. She had easily identified the speakers, but she had been unable to call out because she felt as though the world had begun to whirl round her. Had she not been sitting in the gold velvet chair, she knew that her feeling of sickness would have overwhelmed her, and although not given to fainting spells, she would have had to fight to remain in command of herself.

Suddenly it seemed as though a mask had been ripped from her eyes, and all had become clear to her. So often she had pondered on the real reason why Aidan had wanted her for his bride, and when she asked him, he had merely turned aside and asked in a rather cool voice:

"Do you not know?"

She had shaken her head.

"Why does a gentleman usually offer for a woman he desires as his bride?" he had asked, and she saw a gleam in his eyes.

"I think you tease me," she had replied.

"We will have to get to know one another," he said, "but there is plenty of time. We have a lifetime ahead of us.

There was a lifetime ahead of her, thought Judith sickly, when she would be married to a man who was already in love with his sister-in-law. Yet if Françoise was so practical, why had she not married Aidan in the first place? Surely he was the more wealthy brother?

Colour began to return a little to Judith's cheeks. Had she merely been listening to gossip and malice? She knew that it had not been too well received that Aidan Carrock had chosen herself as his bride when so many people in the county felt that their own daughters were more eligible. At least she could ask Aidan about the mineral deposits. Was her land truly rich? If this were so then . . . then it was likely that the other piece of gossip was also correct, and he loved Françoise.

And she? Françoise was very frank about the fact that she loved both brothers. She had said a short time ago that she loved her husband, but also

Aidan, and wanted him to be happy. And she *had* arranged the wedding . . .

Judith lay back in her chair with closed eyes, hardly able to breathe for the pain in her heart. Suddenly Aidan was beside her once more and leaning over her anxiously.

"Are you unwell, my dear?"

She could not even reply.

"The guests are all positioned in the dining room and we are about to cut the wedding cake," he told her. "Would you feel well enough to do that honour with me? Shall I get you a little wine, then you might feel better?"

Judith made a supreme effort. The guests must not know how she felt. She merely wished the whole day over and for nothing to happen which would make a terrible memory of the day, and cause more gossip.

"I shall manage," she said, huskily. "It will be as you wish."

"I insist upon making your apologies at the earliest opportunity," said Aidan.

"I will not have my wife distressed."

He smiled, but she could not respond. How hollow the words sounded, yet a short time ago they would have filled her heart with such warmth.

She was conducted to her place in the dining room and from then on everything became blurred and hazy. She smiled and nodded, reassured Agnes Laird that she was perfectly happy, and told her that her pale looks were merely fatigue and discomfort from her leg. Mrs. Laird, she suspected, had heard the gossip and had been at great odds with herself as to whether or not to tell Judith. That much was very clear to her now.

But no one must know. No one . . . except Aidan. She would make very sure that *he* knew about the gossip and that she was aware of how she had been duped. No doubt he would tell Françoise. Why, she had actually *liked* Françoise, and it might even be true to say that she had come to love her, even as she had come to love . . .

Judith's heart leapt and hammered.

. . . even as she had come to love Aidan. She could no longer deny the truth of this to herself. He had taken over her life and made her dependent upon him and as her burden had lightened, an inner lightness and joy had been born so that secretly she had looked forward to his visits and had faced her wedding day with an excitement which owed more to a glimpse of great future happiness than to nervousness of the occasion.

Now that it had all been torn away, Judith realised how much it meant to her. She could scarcely believe she had ever considered Mr. Mardale more handsome than Aidan. Today she had hardly sought out Mr. Mardale at all.

But although she wore the heavy rings Aidan had placed upon her finger, she no longer had a sense of belonging to him. Instead her eyes sought Françoise whose cream silk gown was so elegantly styled. She looked like a bride herself. She had pretended that Judith was beautiful but it was Françoise who was beautiful, and who commanded love.

"Do you wish to retire, my dear?" Aidan was whispering in her ear. "You have done all which should be asked of you."

The words put a hard knot of ice round her heart. She had, indeed, done all which should have been asked of her.

"I would like to retire," she said, quietly, and somehow she was taking leave of the guests, and receiving their sympathy for her accident, and good wishes for her full recovery.

In her bedroom Françoise helped Chloe to disrobe her and Judith listened to her artless chatter, then she could no longer dismiss the question uppermost in her mind.

"Françoise, does your husband share this estate with Aidan?"

"Ah, non, non," said Françoise. "My Simon, we do not weesh for Burroughs Park."

"But the wealth . . . "

"So practical," said Françoise, happily. "My Simon, he was heir to his uncle, brother to his mother. Father leaves Burroughs Park to Aidan. Mother's brother leaves his fortune to Simon. He ees wealthy, also. There is no need for you to worry, Judith. It is all arranged very well."

Indeed it *was* all arranged very well! thought Judith as anger began to grow. Aidan had been waiting to come in, and now with a husband's right, he closed the door as Chloe left the room and came over to the bed. The guests had all departed.

"Soon . . . very soon, I hope . . . I shall expect you to occupy your proper bedroom," he said, clearly. His dark face was in shadow as he came to look down on her. "Meantime I am forced to leave you, but I can seal our bargain with a kiss."

He leaned down and his firm lips claimed her own so that Judith's heart beat almost to suffocation.

"No," she whispered. "Do not touch

me. You . . . you know very well why you have married me. Do not pretend that . . . that I mean something to you."

He stiffened. "What are you telling me?"

"Please go," she said, the tears already welling in her eyes. "I . . . I have had enough for now."

"Has it been such an ordeal," he asked, quietly, "to become my wife?"

She did not answer, and moments later he had left the room.

16

FRANÇOISE was unhappy that Judith's recovery had been so retarded by her own wedding that she postponed her trip to London; a decision for which Judith, in her newfound jealousy, gave her very little credit. She and Aidan would no doubt entertain one another very well.

She was cool with Françoise who immediately decided, with concerned innocence, that poor Judith must be in great pain and that she would massage her leg until the pain was encouraged to go.

"You will not touch it," said Judith, sharply. "Please leave me, Françoise. The doctor says I must rest the leg."

"But the blood does not flow well," said Françoise.

"The leg needs the good blood to heal itself. I shall put a leetle oil of olives on my hands and massage the leg. Soon you will be able to walk and make proper wife for our dearest Aidan, no?"

Judith blushed. "No," she said then blushed even more when Françoise surveyed her, suspicion dawning in her eyes.

"You are afraid to be wife to Aidan," she accused. "I would not speak so were we not sisters, but you must not be afraid. I know it is ver' hard for young innocent girl without her mother . . . "

"It is not very hard," said Judith, now scarlet-faced. "I mean, that is *not* why . . . " she bit her lip. "You put words into my mouth Françoise, that I do not wish to say."

"Then what is wrong?"

"My leg must be rested, that is all," said Judith, avoiding her eyes. It was becoming more and more difficult for her to be cold with Françoise. She liked . . . no, she loved Françoise, but she could not help remembering that this was the woman whom Aidan loved. He had only married her for convenience.

Aidan was gentle and solicitous, then he began to look at her suspiciously, just as Françoise had done.

"It occurs to me that you are either sulking, or hiding, my dear Judith," he said, coolly. "There is something here which I do not understand, and I think it refers back to our wedding ceremony. Was there something not quite to your liking? Did I, inadvertently, offend you because I assure you that all was done for your benefit."

"And for that of Françoise," she said, then wished she had held her tongue when he came to tower over her.

"So what is this? he asked, very softly, "what of Françoise? Do I detect a sharpness to your tongue?"

"I learned the *true* reason why you married me, as I sat in my chair after the wedding ceremony," she said, goaded. "I learned that you . . . you loved Françoise and she had . . . had loved you, but . . . but had married Simon."

His face had gone very pale and his eyes glittered. He drew a chair up beside her and looked closely into her face.

"Why, I wonder, would Françoise marry my brother if she were in love with me?"

"She is French. She is very practical," said Judith, beginning to feel wretched, but unable to stop herself from voicing all her own jealous thoughts. "He is very rich, being heir to his uncle."

The colour began to return to his face, until it burned brightly in his cheeks.

"It *is* gossip which you repeat, is it not? I recognise the tone of these words. From whom did you hear this . . . these facts?"

"There was more," she said, her own temper rising. "It would seem that I am not so penniless as I had feared. You were very eager to buy my land, but now I understand that the rich mineral deposits reach towards Greyfells and not Burroughs Park."

"From whom did you hear this gossip?" he repeated, rapping a small table loudly on this last word. She could see that he was furiously angry.

"The wives of two of our neighbours . . . Mrs. Westworth of Foxenholm and Lady Darval."

He turned to stare out of the window, but his whole body seemed to quiver with rage. She began to feel sick with nerves, and she had to gather her courage together. The position must be made plain.

"Do you deny that you love Françoise?" she asked, carefully.

"No."

"Do you deny that there are mineral deposits under Greyfells?"

"I deny none of it," he said, silkily, turning to her once again with the movements of a jungle animal. She flinched, feeling that he was about to strike her.

"But if you, madam, listen so

carefully to the gossip of two evil-tongued old women without asking for my own opinions, then you are not *fit* to be mistress of Burroughs Park. I love my sister-in-law and foolishly believed that you love her, too. There *are* hopes of some mineral deposits under Greyfells, but it has yet to be shown whether or not it is rich, or whether the seam will run out. My mining activities have not as yet progressed *so* far, as you should very well know. I had thought you would be pleased to have a man running your affairs and taking such responsibilities from your young shoulders . . . " again he thumped the table, " . . . and I imagined that you had the intelligence to see this and that we . . . we might come to have a good . . . " He paused as though searching for a word, " . . . a good relationship one day, even if you cannot give me your love.

"Many very good marriages are without love when the contract is made. I do not blame you if you do not love me. But I am deeply angered that you should allow sour-tongued malice such importance in your judgements. Do you not understand why I insisted upon a fine wedding when a quick visit from our Vicar would have been more to my liking? Because I did not want our neighbours ever to remember that we married thus. I wanted them to *know* I was proud of my bride. I wanted you to have the finest of gowns and for them to see you as I see you . . . *saw* you," he corrected.

There was a great tight knot in Judith's chest, so that she could not even speak. Yet through it all she could only think of one thing. He had admitted to loving Françoise, but he had spoken as though he loved her as a sister. And she felt mean and greedy for wealth when he explained that the mineral ores *might* be under Greyfells, but it was not certain. Like all gossip, it had only shown part of the truth.

"I . . . I am sorry," she whispered. "Perhaps I have been wrong."

He sat down in the chair near the window, and was silent for so long that she felt he had not heard. Then he turned to her.

"No, it is my fault. I expected too much of you. You are the elder sister and in the absence of relatives, you have had charge of your own affairs, but one forgets that you are still very young . . . a mere child."

This new tone was the most humiliating of all. She was *not* a child, but she could see now how foolish and childish she had been. Yet how could she be blamed? He had never explained to her true satisfaction why he had chosen her from a dozen more eligible girls. The gossip had appeared to answer her doubts so plausibly.

He did not love her. When he had first asked her to marry him, he had said, quite clearly, that they need not concern themselves with love. Now it seemed to her that he did not even like her whilst she . . . she loved him now beyond anything. How could she try to make him see that it was only her jealousy which made her believe those things about Françoise? She would have to explain her own love for him in order to make him understand, and even then he would look upon her with contempt. Françoise had been so kind to her, yet she had thrown that kindness in her face. And she *did* love Françoise. She loved her very much.

Tears had gathered in her eyes and began to slide down her cheeks and he leapt to his feet.

"Do not weep," he said, gruffly. "We have a sad tangle since it is apparent to me that you find our marriage abhorrent. I made an error of judgement." He stared at her, deep in thought. "I will leave you to rest."

The door closed behind him and she no longer tried to stem the hot tears as they slid down her cheeks. But they were not healing tears, and she knew that she had never been so unhappy in her life.

17

FRANÇOISE departed for London along with her mother and Chloe, and Mrs. Whitaker, the elderly housekeeper who had been employed at Burroughs Park for some years, assumed the task of caring for Judith and she appointed two of the maids to attend to her.

"If you have any special wishes, ma'am," she said to Judith, "I will do my best to see that they are carried out. Jane Greenlaw is a fine nurse. She will help in the healing of your leg."

"It is much better," said Judith. "I only require that Jane shall help me with simple exercises each day."

She no longer desired to remain in her bedroom and felt very much at a disadvantage because she was unable to move about as freely as she wished.

Aidan was very busy because of the

progress of the mine and worked long hours with his estate manager, Joseph Webb. She saw little of him, but for a short period each day when he inquired politely for her health, then took his leave of her.

Even after Judith began to move around the house with the aid of a stick, there was no suggestion that she should move to the master bedroom. She was quite sharp with Mrs. Whitaker when the housekeeper hinted that such a move could be made very soon and thereafter Mrs. Whitaker held her peace, though her eyes were questioning as she looked at her master and his young bride. This was not a very good start to a marriage in her opinion.

Judith missed Françoise much more than she could ever have possibly imagined, but she was happy to welcome Bess who had pleaded to be allowed to stay at Greyfells instead of Burroughs Park and who sometimes walked over to see her. Bess, however, had a look of displeasure on her face and it was not hard to guess that something was upsetting her.

"I think it a great pity that you should change your mind about Greyfells, sister," she said, a trifle huffily. "I would have thought Burroughs Park large enough and fine enough for any woman. No one can say you are not the fine lady, living as you do at Burroughs."

She looked with jealousy at Judith's charming primrose yellow and white gown, one of a wardrobe of clothes which Françoise had ordered for her, and which Aidan insisted that she wore.

"You may have callers," he told her. "I expect you to wear gowns in keeping with your position."

She had agreed without fuss, and now, apart from her paler complexion and a certain lack of sparkle in her eyes, Bess thought that her sister looked very well indeed.

"I am comfortable," Judith told her.

"What has happened at Greyfells?"

"Nothing has happened," said Bess, "but Colonel Mardale and his wife are coming home from India and hope to take up residence at Hazlemont."

"But how splendid!" said Judith, wondering why this should upset Bess.

"They wish to live there permanently now that Colonel Mardale's parents are so elderly and so frail. Jonathan hoped that we could live at Hazlemont after our marriage, but because his parents wish to return home, it would not be convenient. We consulted Mr. Carrock . . . your husband, Judith . . . and asked that we might live at Greyfells. Jonathan would be happy to manage the place. At first Mr. Carrock appeared to favour such a request, but now he says the matter must be considered more carefully. You might have other plans for Greyfells. *What* plans, sister? Surely you cannot wish to live there yourself, ever, again? Why should you want Greyfells?"

Judith's cheeks had coloured. Did

Aidan plan to return her to Greyfells? Was he even now trying to have their marriage annulled?

"I do not see why you should wish to occupy two homes," Bess pursued. "Could you not speak to Mr. Carrock and ask him to reconsider? Greyfells is in need of management and Jonathan would be happy to offer his services. Nothing could be more fitting since he will not be needed at Hazlemont."

It *was* a good idea, thought Judith. She would feel much better about Greyfells if Bess lived there permanently after her marriage to Mr. Mardale.

"I will see what I can do," she promised.

"I would not have thought you so meek and mild with Mr. Carrock," said Bess, rather curiously. "I had expected you to argue with him despite the fact that he is a hard man. But you were also a hard woman, Judith. Perhaps you do not know it, but you were. Can it be that now you . . . you are afraid of him?"

"No, of course not," she said, crossly. "I still have not recovered completely from the accident. That is all."

"They do say that Françoise was his mistress," said Bess, in a whisper, looking round furtively to see that she was not overheard. "I hesitate to tell you, but I feel you should know."

"Who says so?"

"It is all the gossip, sister."

"I hope you will play your part in denying such gossip," said Judith.

"Then it is untrue?"

"Certainly it is untrue."

Judith stared at her sister, proudly, then rose as Bess decided to take her leave. She walked over to close a window against a capricious wind and saw Aidan striding away from the window. Had he heard? she wondered. But of course he could not have heard. Bess had spoken in whispers, and she had not spoken out very strongly.

Yet she felt uneasy that her sister was now repeating such gossip.

As Judith's health returned to normal she became increasingly unhappy with her situation. Her marriage was no marriage and she knew that this state of affairs could not last for long. Aidan Carrock needed a wife, and an heir to his fine estate and other business interests. Her pride made her want to return home, quietly, to Greyfells and for him to have their marriage annulled, but Bess grew more and more sulky that no decision was being made about appointing Jonathan Mardale to manage Greyfells. Their wedding was being arranged for late autumn and Bess was unhappy that she might be obliged to live at Hazlemont, however temporary. She found that Jonathan's parents, on their return home, were still deeply concerned about Indian affairs, and they had no points of common interest with their son's prospective bride.

Judith had not been able to resist

concerning herself with the running of Burroughs Park, and Mrs. Whitaker was apparently glad to hand over the reins to the new mistress. Since it might not always be her home, Judith had been circumspect about making changes, but it was easy to forget that she was mistress in name only, and to carry on with the much needed improvements which Françoise had instigated. There were many more rooms still requiring to be refurbished.

She did not think that Aidan had noticed her efforts, but one afternoon he arrived home unexpectedly from a business journey to Carlisle and found Judith, with the assistance of two maidservants, investigating the contents of a large dark storage cupboard. She wore a large white overall over her sprigged muslin gown, and her face and hands had become soiled as she and the maidservants lifted out splendid sets of china for dinnerware, and much tarnished, but elegantly styled silverware.

Aidan's glance was cold as she stood back in some confusion, and quickly she ordered the maidservants to carry several of the silver pieces to the kitchen for cleaning.

"I would prefer that you consult Mrs. Whitaker with regard to kitchen affairs," he told her. "You might have unexpected guests, and I do not wish them to find my wife in disarray."

Judith's temper had also returned along with her good health.

"Wife?" she asked. "I am no wife to you, Mr. Carrock, and you know it very well. As to my looks, it is easy to remove a pinafore." She proceeded to whip it off. "My gown is *not* that of a servant."

His mouth twisted and for a moment she thought that he was stifling laughter.

"And are these hands also in keeping with the mistress of Burroughs Park?"

Her hands were no longer work worn, but they were streaked with dirt, though she had no notion that her face was equally dirty.

"They can quickly be washed, sir. It is disgraceful, however, that such beautiful china and silverware should lie forgotten and hidden in this cupboard. It should be put into daily use and . . . and enjoyed."

"Then we must talk about it," he decided, leading her towards a small morning room which she liked to use. "In here, perhaps. You are in no fit state to grace the drawing room."

She flushed, but her temper was now well tried, and it was an easy matter to brooch the subject of Greyfells.

"My sister has called to see me," she began and he inclined his head.

"So?"

"So she wishes to have a decision about Greyfells, as to whether or not Mr. Mardale will be asked to manage the estate. Is it true that more mineral deposits have been found on another part of our land?"

"Very true," he said, coolly, "and Mardale would be an excellent choice as manager of the estate. It could prove quite rich in ore, and would put the estate on to a good footing." He paused for a moment. "I would like to have *your* opinion on this matter."

Her lips felt dry. "In what way?"

"I do not think it requires to be clarified. I would welcome your thoughts on your own future. Do you want your sister to live at Greyfells when she marries Mardale? Now that it is prosperous and there is no need for the delicate boys, will you not wish to return there yourself, and you will not find it . . . ah . . . uncomfortable as you try to prevent yourself from languishing after Mardale . . . your own sister's husband? Because that is the choice, my dear Judith. If you remain here, then you instruct Mrs. Whitaker to move your personal possessions to the master bedroom which you must be prepared to share with *me*. You were quite right. You are no wife to me, and the situation cannot wait any longer."

The warm colour rushed to her

cheeks. He always made her feel that everything was her fault, but it was he who had married her under false pretences. He still loved Françoise.

"Is it your experience that languishing after one's brother-in-law *or* sister-in-law brings a great deal of unhappiness?" she asked.

The gleam of light left his eyes and he gripped her arm.

"Now that you are fully recovered, madam, it might be helpful if I spanked you. I love my sister-in-law as a sister. Nothing more. But if you cannot stop sighing for the attentions of Mardale . . . "

"I do *not* sigh for his attentions!" she cried. "I admit I admired Mr. Mardale when we first met, but I have long since accepted him as my future brother-in-law and have a mere fondness for him. I can only be happy for my sister and her husband, when they marry. My sadness is that . . . that such happiness has been denied us," she ended in a low voice.

He was very still, then he sighed deeply and came to take her hand, examining it closely as he had done in the past.

"My poor little Judith," he said, tenderly. "You are still little more than a child, yet you have had so many worries and disappointments. It is very sad because I wanted to give you so much. I just want you to be happy."

Her eyes were wide as she looked at him.

"But why should you concern yourself about me?" she asked.

"Why? Because I love you, of course. Why else would I want to marry you? Surely I have explained all that to you . . . "

"You did not!" she said, quickly, though her face was becoming transfigured with happiness. Aidan loved her! He had married her because he loved her!

He cupped her cheeks with his hands and looked down into her shining eyes.

"What is this?" he asked, softly. "No

sulky looks because I have reminded you that you are my wife?"

"Oh, Aidan," she whispered, "I am so glad that I am your wife, if you truly love me. You did not say so before and . . . and I have been so jealous of Françoise, even though I do love her. I would be happy to have her as a sister."

His fingers caressed her cheeks.

"I cannot believe what I hear, that you love me? I thought that your heart was given to Mardale."

"Not as I love you," she said, earnestly. "I was so hurt when the gossips said you loved Françoise and only wanted me for the mineral rights and because I . . . I was not likely to mind . . . about Françoise, that is. They said that the French have liberal ideas about . . . about love and marriage, but I could not have it so. I wanted you for myself."

"Oh, Judith! What a price that would have been to pay for a few wagon loads of lead ore! And surely Françoise has

265

never hidden the fact that she and my brother are very happy in their marriage. She admires him, as well as being in love with him and they are an ideally happy couple."

He had drawn her into his arms.

"Does this mean that you wish to be my wife in all respects."

She blushed but her eyes held his.

"Whatever you wish, Aidan."

"I cannot believe that you will always be so agreeable." This time he did not hide the laughter in his eyes, then he bent to kiss her and the world became a place vibrant with happiness for both of them.

"I am so happy," she said as she leaned against his shoulder.

"And I am in doubt as to whether my face has remained clean after kissing you. There is dirt on your cheek and on your forehead."

"Oh dear, I shall never know why you find me attractive," she said, trying to pull away. But his arms tightened about her.

"Do you not, little one?" he asked tenderly, "yet you are the most beautiful, most courageous girl I have ever known. You have given me hours of misery when I thought you would never turn to me, but we will make up for the early days of our marriage as soon as possible."

"I would like Françoise and Simon to come back," she said. "I feel I have not been as loving to her as I might . . . as I want to be. I want her to know that I am sorry, and that I appreciate all that she did for me."

"They have gone back Martinique, but there is no reason why we cannot go to see them. Would that please you, my dearest wife?"

Judith's eyes shone like twin sapphires.

"Oh, Aidan, it would. I cannot believe that I am so happy."

"Let us hope our sons will not be delicate," he said, and his voice was rich with laughter.

WITH SOMEBODY ELSE
Theresa Charles

Rosamond sets off for Cornwall with Hugo to meet his family, blissfully unaware of the shocks in store for her.

A SUMMER FOR STRANGERS
Claire Hamilton

Because she had lost her job, her flat and she had no money, Tabitha agreed to pose as Adam's future wife although she believed the scheme to be deceitful and cruel.

VILLA OF SINGING WATER
Angela Petron

The disquieting incidents that occurred at the Vatican and the Colosseum did not trouble Jan at first, but then they became increasingly unpleasant and alarming.

DOCTOR NAPIER'S NURSE
Pauline Ash

When cousins Midge and Derry are entered as probationer nurses on the same day but at different hospitals they agree to exchange identities.

A GIRL LIKE JULIE
Louise Ellis

Caroline absolutely adored Hugh Barrington, but then Julie Crane came into their lives. Julie was the kind of girl who attracts men without even trying.

COUNTRY DOCTOR
Paula Lindsay

When Evan Richmond bought a practice in a remote country village he did not realise that a casual encounter would lead to the loss of his heart.

ENCORE
Helga Moray

Craig and Janet realise that their true happiness lies with each other, but it is only under traumatic circumstances that they can be reunited.

NICOLETTE
Ivy Preston

When Grant Alston came back into her life, Nicolette was faced with a dilemma. Should she follow the path of duty or the path of love?

THE GOLDEN PUMA
Margaret Way

Catherine's time was spent looking after her father's Queensland farm. But what life was there without David, who wasn't interested in her?

HOSPITAL BY THE LAKE
Anne Durham

Nurse Marguerite Ingleby was always ready to become personally involved with her patients, to the despair of Brian Field, the Senior Surgical Registrar, who loved her.

VALLEY OF CONFLICT
David Farrell

Isolated in a hostel in the French Alps, Ann Russell sees her fiancé being seduced by a young girl. Then comes the avalanche that imperils their lives.

NURSE'S CHOICE
Peggy Gaddis

A proposal of marriage from the incredibly handsome and wealthy Reagan was enough to upset any girl — and Brooke Martin was no exception.

A DANGEROUS MAN
Anne Goring

Photographer Polly Burton was on safari in Mombasa when she met enigmatic Leon Hammond. But unpredictability was the name of the game where Leon was concerned.

PRECIOUS INHERITANCE
Joan Moules

Karen's new life working for an authoress took her from Sussex to a foreign airstrip and a kidnapping; to a real life adventure as gripping as any in the books she typed.

VISION OF LOVE
Grace Richmond

When Kathy takes over the rundown country kennels she finds Alec Stinton, a local vet, very helpful. But their friendship arouses bitter jealousy and a tragedy seems inevitable.

CRUSADING NURSE
Jane Converse

It was handsome Dr. Corbett who opened Nurse Susan Leighton's eyes and who set her off on a lonely crusade against some powerful enemies and a shattering struggle against the man she loved.

WILD ENCHANTMENT
Christina Green

Rowan's agreeable new boss had a dream of creating a famous perfume using her precious Silverstar, but Rowan's plans were very different.

DESERT ROMANCE
Irene Ord

Sally agrees to take her sister Pam's place as La Chartreuse the dancer, but she finds out there is more to it than dyeing her hair red and looking like her sister.

HEART OF ICE
Marie Sidney

How was January to know that not only would the warmth of the Swiss people thaw out her frozen heart, but that she too would play her part in helping someone to live again?

LUCKY IN LOVE
Margaret Wood

Companion-secretary to wealthy gambler Laura Duxford, who lived in Monaco, seemed to Melanie a fabulous job. Especially as Melanie had already lost her heart to Laura's son, Julian.

NURSE TO PRINCESS JASMINE
Lilian Woodward

Nick's surgeon brother, Tom, performs an operation on an Arabian princess, and she invites Tom, Nick and his fiancé to Omander, where a web of deceit and intrigue closes about them.

THE WAYWARD HEART
Eileen Barry

Disaster-prone Katherine's nickname was "Kate Calamity", but her boss went too far with an outrageous proposal, which because of her latest disaster, she could not refuse.

FOUR WEEKS IN WINTER
Jane Donnelly

Tessa wasn't looking forward to meeting Paul Mellor again — she had made a fool of herself over him once before. But was Orme Jared's solution to her problem likely to be the right one?

SURGERY BY THE SEA
Sheila Douglas

Medical student Meg hadn't really wanted to go and work with a G.P. on the Welsh coast although the job had its compensations. But Owen Roberts was certainly not one of them!

HEAVEN IS HIGH
Anne Hampson

The new heir to the Manor of Marbeck had been found. But it was rather unfortunate that when he arrived unexpectedly he found an uninvited guest, complete with stetson and high boots.

LOVE WILL COME
Sarah Devon

June Baker's boss was not really her idea of her ideal man, but when she went from third typist to boss's secretary overnight she began to change her mind.

ESCAPE TO ROMANCE
Kay Winchester

Oliver and Jean first met on Swale Island. They were both trying to begin their lives afresh, but neither had bargained for complications from the past.

CASTLE IN THE SUN
Cora Mayne

Emma's invalid sister, Kym, needed a warm climate, and Emma jumped at the chance of a job on a Mediterranean island. But Emma soon finds that intrigues and hazards lurk on the sunlit isle.

BEWARE OF LOVE
Kay Winchester

Carol Brampton resumes her nursing career when her family is killed in a car accident. With Dr. Patrick Farrell she begins to pick up the pieces of her life, but is bitterly hurt when insinuations are made about her to Patrick.

DARLING REBEL
Sarah Devon

When Jason Farradale's secretary met with an accident, her glamorous stand-in was quite unable to deal with one problem in particular.

THE PRICE OF PARADISE
Jane Arbor

It was a shock to Fern to meet her estranged husband on an island in the middle of the Indian Ocean, but to discover that her father had engineered it puzzled Fern. What did he hope to achieve?

DOCTOR IN PLASTER
Lisa Cooper

When Dr. Scott Sutcliffe is injured, Nurse Caroline Hurst has to cope with a very demanding private case. But when she realises her exasperating patient has stolen her heart, how can Caroline possibly stay?

A TOUCH OF HONEY
Lucy Gillen

Before she took the job as secretary to author Robert Dean, Cadie had heard how charming he was, but that wasn't her first impression at all.

ROMANTIC LEGACY
Cora Mayne

As kennelmaid to the Armstrongs, Ann Brown, had no idea that she would become the central figure in a web of mystery and intrigue.

THE RELENTLESS TIDE
Jill Murray

Steve Palmer shared Nurse Marie Blane's love of the sea and small boats. Marie's other passion was her step-brother. But when danger threatened who should she turn to — her step-brother or the man who stirred emotions in her heart?

ROMANCE IN NORWAY
Cora Mayne

Nancy Crawford hopes that her visit to Norway will help her to start life again. She certainly finds many surprises there, including unexpected happiness.

UNLOCK MY HEART
Honor Vincent

When Ruth Linton, a young widow with three children, inherits a house in the country, it seems to be the answer to her dreams. But Ruth's problems were only just beginning . . .

SWEET PROMISE
Janet Dailey

Erica had met Rafael in Mexico, where their relationship had been brief but dramatic. Now, over a year later in Texas, she had met him again — and he had the power to wreck her life.

SAFARI ENCOUNTER
Rosemary Carter

Jenny had to accept that she couldn't run her father's game park alone; so she let forceful Joshua Adams virtually take over. But Joshua took over her heart as well!

W
in
wa
as
re
hi

1 21 41 61 81 101 121 141 161 181
2 22 42 62 82 102 122 142 162 182
3 23 43 63 83 103 123 143 163 183
4 24 44 64 84 104 124 144 164 184
5 25 45 65 85 105 125 145 165 185
6 26 46 66 86 106 126 146 166 186
7 27 47 67 87 107 127 147 167 187
8 28 48 68 88 108 128 148 168 188
9 29 49 69 89 109 129 149 169 189
10 30 50 70 90 110 130 150 170 190
11 31 51 71 91 111 131 151 171 191
12 32 52 72 92 112 132 152 172 192
13 33 53 73 93 113 133 153 173 193
14 34 54 74 94 114 134 154 174 194
15 (35) 55 75 95 115 135 155 175 195
16 36 56 76 96 116 136 156 176 196
17 37 57 77 97 117 137 157 177 197
18 38 58 78 98 118 138 158 178 198
19 39 59 79 99 119 139 159 179 199
20 40 60 80 100 120 140 160 180 200

"
d
P
E
n
S
S
I
t
t
t
'

201 221 241 261 281 301 321 341 361 381
202 222 242 262 282 302 322 342 362 382
203 223 243 263 283 303 (323) 343 363 383
204 224 244 264 284 304 324 344 364 384
205 225 245 265 285 305 325 345 365 385
206 226 246 266 286 306 326 346 366 386
207 227 247 267 287 307 327 347 367 387
208 228 248 268 288 308 328 348 368 388
209 229 249 269 289 309 329 349 369 389
210 230 250 270 290 310 330 350 370 390
211 231 251 271 291 311 331 351 371 391
212 232 252 272 292 312 332 352 372 392
213 233 253 273 293 313 333 353 373 393
214 234 254 274 294 314 334 354 374 394
215 235 255 275 295 315 335 355 375 395
216 236 256 276 296 316 336 356 376 396
(217) 237 257 277 297 317 337 357 377 397
218 238 258 278 298 318 338 358 378 398
219 239 259 279 299 319 339 359 379 399
220 240 260 280 300 320 340 360 380 400